MAN HUNTING

Kate smiled smugly at Jake. "I have a date this afternoon."

"Oh, Lord." Jake closed his eyes. "Who are you going to destroy now?"

"I beg your pardon?"

"The resort would appreciate it if you'd just throw back the men you don't want without maiming them."

"I haven't maimed anyone," Kate protested.

"You almost drowned Lance. You scared Peter into heart palpitations. You hit Brad over the head with a bottle." Jake shook his head. "And you still have men asking you out?"

"Lance grabbed me. Peter was cheating at golf. And, I might point out, I hit Brad to save you."

Jake gave her a wicked grin. "Has *any guy* actually finished a date with you?"

Watch for JENNIFER CRUSIE's
GET RID OF BRADLEY

Coming November 2001
From MIRA Books

Jennifer Crusie

MAN HUNTING

MIRA

ISBN 1-55166-618-9

MANHUNTING

Copyright © 1993 by Jennifer Crusie.

Visit us at www.mirabooks.com

Printed in U.S.A.

For Sherie Posesorski,
who has the steadfastness of Ruth,
the patience of Job
and the cutting skills of Judith.

And for Mollie Amanda Smith,
the most amazing woman I know.

One

"Planning on jumping? I wouldn't. Blood's hell to get out of silk."

"I'm just checking the weather," Kate Svenson said patiently and continued to stare out her apartment window, knowing that Jessie would lose interest and go back to her newspaper if she ignored her long enough.

She'd pulled back the thick drapes to let in the early-morning August sun. Even with her best friend sitting behind her, rustling her paper and slurping her coffee, Kate felt alone, mired in a despair that not even Jessie's pragmatism could dispel. *This is doing you no good at all,* she told herself and moved away from the window to sit at her linen-covered dining-room table. She tried to concentrate on her breakfast coffee and the business section of the Sunday paper, but her mind kept wandering to the miserable state of her life.

Well, not exactly miserable, she thought. *Actually, not miserable at all. I have a great career in a top management-consulting firm. Of course, I could wish that my father didn't own the firm, and sometimes it's boring, but it's a great career— Well, an okay career....*

With an effort, Kate pushed her career out of her mind and went on with her catalog of blessings. Her life was good. She had her health, and enough money, and terrific friends, the best of whom she was having breakfast with right now in a beautiful apartment full of exquisite French Provincial furniture that she certainly couldn't afford if she didn't have this damn job....

No. Kate clamped down on her negative thoughts and peered over the top of her paper at the brunette across from her who was reading her paper and drinking her coffee with the same total absorption she gave everything else.

Jessie Rogers jerked her head up, her dark curls bouncing. "What?"

"Nothing," Kate said. "Just counting my blessings. You're near the top."

"I *am* the top, which is a real comment on your lousy life," Jessie said and went back to the paper.

Trust Jessie to cut to the chase, Kate thought. *She sits over there looking like Audrey Hepburn at twelve, and here I am looking like Grace Kelly at fifty. And we're both thirty-five. Doesn't she care that life is slipping away from us while we carve out careers we don't want?*

Of course, Jessie didn't care. Her life wasn't slipping away, she was living it. She wasn't carving out a career she didn't want, she was completely involved in one she loved, if you could call cake decorating a career, which of course, Jessie did, although how she lived on it, Kate would never know. Jessie just went with the flow, no plan at all. Maybe if Kate hadn't planned her career out so precisely, maybe if she was doing something else...

Stop it, she told herself. She was a damn good management consultant, and she'd made a lot of money. It wasn't her career that was bothering her, it was her empty personal life. Of course, Jessie was happier than she was. She hadn't gotten herself into three horrible engagements in the past three years because she didn't care that she was thirty-five and not married. *I'm the one who cares,*

Kate thought. She was the one who was guilty and miserable. It shouldn't matter but it did, and there was nothing she could do about it.

Pathetic. Kate sighed and went back to her paper.

Jessie slapped the newspaper down on the linen-covered tabletop and said loudly, "This is all your father's fault."

Startled, Kate looked up from the paper. "What? The recession? The construction on 70? Calvin can't find Hobbes? What?"

"Don't play dumb." Jessie folded her arms and glared at her. "You're unhappy."

"No, I'm not," Kate said, forcing a smile. "You read that in the paper? What are you reading? I told you not to read the personals. You get too upset about all the lonely people and you transfer it to me. I'm fine. Read the sports page." She went back to her paper, holding it like a shield in front of her.

Jessie, as usual, did not give up. "You keep sighing. I can't concentrate on Travel and Leisure with you sighing."

"I'm not sighing," Kate said without looking up. "It's sinus."

"No, it's not." Jessie narrowed her eyes. "You're not still pining over that jerk Derek, are you?"

"No." Kate stuck to her paper. "I don't pine over jerks. It's not time-efficient. Go back to Travel and Leisure."

Jessie hooked her finger over the edge of Kate's paper and pulled it down so she could look into her friend's eyes. "You want to get married."

"Of course I want to get married," Kate said reasonably. "Some day. Get your finger off my paper. You're crumpling the Dow-Jones."

"You want to get married now." Jessie looked disgusted. "It's your biological clock or something."

"Your nail polish is chipped," Kate said. "It's also a really ugly color, but I'm not mentioning that because it would be none of my business."

"You've been engaged three times in the past three years," Jessie said. "Not one of them could keep you. You said yes to three men and then dumped them. Why would you say 'yes' to three men you couldn't bring yourself to marry?"

Kate took a deep breath. "Derek insisted on a premarital agreement. Paul informed me that my success threatened him and if I loved him I'd stop working so hard. Terence wanted me to quit my job because my social duties as his wife would be too pressing. And you think I should have married one of those men?"

"Frankly, I don't think you should have *dated* any of them," Jessie said. "I just think being raised by your father has given you a warped idea of life, marriage, and men. And I think you're unhappy, which makes me unhappy. And I don't like being unhappy, so we're going to fix you."

Kate put down the financial section. "No, we're not."

"Yes, we are," Jessie said. "We're going to improve your life. We're going to make you more like me."

Kate started to laugh. "I don't want to be like you."

"Hey," Jessie said, not fazed at all. "You should be so lucky."

"You decorate cakes for a living," Kate said. "Beautiful cakes, admittedly, but still…"

"I'm an artist," Jessie said.

"You're a nut," Kate said. "But I love you, so I overlook it."

"I may be nuts, but I love what I do and you don't,"

Jessie said. "Remember when you were with the Small Business Administration? You used to tell me about all those little businesses you'd help get started, and you'd feel so good, remember?"

"The pay was terrible and the career possibilities nil." Kate picked up her paper. Jessie pinned it down with her hand.

"Remember Mrs. Borden's day-care center?" Jessie said. "It's still going strong. She's got a waiting list."

"Of course, I remember." Kate smiled at the memory. "What a lovely woman she was."

"Is," Jessie said. "She didn't die just because you sold out."

"I didn't sell out—"

"And that old man—what was his name, Richards? The one with the shoe-repair shop."

"Richter," Kate said. "Mr. Richter. How is he?"

Jessie shrugged. "How should I know? Like it's my job to keep an eye on all those little businesses you played midwife to."

"Very subtle, Jess," Kate said. "And I didn't sell out—I'm doing the same thing." At Jessie's skeptical look, she added, "I am. I'm just saving much bigger businesses for a lot more money. I'm still helping people."

"You're helping a bunch of suits," Jessie said.

Kate held on to her patience. "Why don't we just agree that we have no respect for each other's career choices and forget the whole thing?"

"You used to have respect for my career choice," Jessie said. "You helped me save my career."

"I couldn't help it," Kate said. "You were such a mess, standing in the middle of my office at the SBA, raving about creating the greatest cakes in the civilized world.'' She smiled at Jessie and shook her head. ''I'd never seen anyone like you before.''

Jessie grinned back. ''I felt the same way. I'd never seen anybody as polished as you. You looked like you'd been varnished. I thought, *Oh, good, I'm in big trouble and they send me to Wall Street Barbie.*'' She tilted her head and looked at Kate with deep affection. ''And then you saved my business.''

''It was a business worth saving,'' Kate said. ''You truly do make the most beautiful cakes in the civilized world.''

''Uncivilized, too,'' Jessie said. ''Which brings us to the subject at hand—men.''

''Jessie,'' Kate said. ''You're even more inept with men than I am. You keep dating those boneless, purposeless men who need someone to take care of them.''

''Yes, but that's because I don't care,'' Jessie said. ''When I care, I will be ept.''

''Well, when you're ept, I'll listen to you.'' Kate tried to pick up her paper, but Jessie put her hand on it again.

''Listen,'' Jessie said, leaning forward. ''I'm willing to approach this your way.''

''My way?''

''Right. Logic and reason.'' Jessie made a face. ''I prefer instinct, but we've gotta go with what we've got, here. Now, you want to get married, right?''

Kate looked wary. ''Right.''

Jessie spread her hands apart. ''So what have you done all your life every time you wanted something?''

Kate looked even warier. ''I made a plan?''

''Exactly,'' Jessie said. ''So we make a plan. What do we do first? I've never planned anything before, remember? You were the one who came in and did my business plan." She stopped to consider. "Which means I *owe* you this plan. It's the least I can do."

"The least is what you always do," Kate said. "If you'd followed the timetable in that plan, you'd be a rich woman today. What happened to all the promotion plans? The growth plans?"

"Too fast," Jessie said, waving the idea away with her hand. "If I'd stuck to your timetable, I'd have lost all the fun of designing the cakes. I'd end up turning out sugar roses like a robot, and after a while all my work would look like everybody else's, and nobody would be paying my prices, so I'd have to lower them, and then I'd have to make more cakes to cover the loss, and then they'd get really ugly, and I'd go out of business and starve." She looked at Kate triumphantly.

"You just don't want to succeed," Kate said. "You just want to noodle around with sugar, having a good time."

"And you want to succeed too much," Jessie said, leaning forward again as she closed in on her point. "You think you just want to make money, and having a good time doesn't matter. But it does, honey, and that's why you're miserable today. And I'm not. And I don't noodle. I'm an artist."

"Jessie..." Kate began, but Jessie overrode her.

"Come on. How do we start making a plan?"

Kate sighed and decided that humoring Jessie was easier than fighting her. "Well, first, you have to set goals."

"Okay." Jessie reached down and fished in her floppy embroidered bag for a pencil. While she was searching, Kate stood, walked over to her writing table, picked up a gold Cross pen, walked back, and handed it to Jessie.

"Thanks," Jessie said, dropping her bag. "I've got to

clean out this purse. Make sure I give this back. I forget and keep them all the time.''

''I know,'' Kate said, sitting down again.

''Now, what is your goal? To find Mr. Right and get married, right?''

''Right.'' Kate moved Jessie's paper aside to find her coffee cup.

''So what kind of prospects are we looking for, here?''

The edge of Jessie's paper had flopped into her cup, so Kate pulled it out, blotting it with a napkin so it wouldn't stain her tablecloth. ''Your newspaper was in my coffee.''

''Sorry.'' Jessie pulled the paper aside and began to write in the white space of a Bank One ad. ''Number one, he has to be rich.''

''He does not,'' Kate said. ''I'm not mercenary.''

Jessie looked up at her patiently. ''No, but your daddy's rich and your stepmom's goodlookin'. Being poor is what sank Derek-who-wanted-a-premarital, remember? You've got to find somebody who's got more than you're going to inherit.''

''Janice is not that good-looking. And she will probably be doing the inheriting.'' *Unless Dad moves on to wife number six.*

Jessie waved Kate's objection away. ''You're just jealous because she's ten years younger than you are. Okay. Number two. He has to be older than you by about, oh, fifteen years.''

''Why?'' Kate asked, mystified.

''Because you're obviously looking for a father figure.''

''I am not. Give me that.'' Kate took the paper away from Jessie and crossed out one and two. ''All right. One, he has to be intelligent. Very, very intelligent.''

"Intelligent's good," Jessie said, grinning.

"And not only the academic kind of intelligence. He has to be, well, *discerning*. He has to…know quality."

"Look for the designer label?" Jessie made a face. "This is your dream man?"

"And distinguished," Kate said, caught up in the plan. "Well-mannered. Someone who would be comfortable at the opera."

"You hate opera."

Kate waved the objection away. "And aggressive. He has to know what he wants and go after it."

"Okay." Jessie picked up her coffee cup and tried to drink while Kate worked. The cup was empty so she swapped it for Kate's.

"And successful. He has to be successful."

"In whose eyes?"

"What?" Kate looked up, distracted.

"Well," Jessie said reasonably, "different people define success different ways."

"Making at least four times his age, with the same in blue chips." Kate spoke automatically, barely aware of what she was saying as she went back to her list.

"Sounds like a quote," Jessie said. "Now let me guess who said it first? Shakespeare? Naw. Mark Twain? Naw. Wait. Wait. I've got it. Bertram Svenson, father of the year."

"What?"

"So have we got to the good stuff yet?" Jessie asked.

"What good stuff?"

"Great sense of humor. Equal rights for women. Terrific in bed. Loves you to the point of madness."

"Well, yes, of course." Kate looked down at her list. "Did I mention successful?"

"Several times." Jessie took the paper back. "Okay,

we have the animal defined. Now, what's the next move? To find him, right?''

"Right." Kate picked up her coffee cup, frowning when she saw it was empty. "Did you drink my coffee?''

"Yes. I was feeling aggressive. Now, your next step is to find a hunting ground.''

"Jessie, I don't…''

Jessie held up her hand. "Which I have already found for you." She carefully tore Kate's list out of the paper and handed it to her. "Keep that." Then she turned back to the Travel and Leisure section. "Look at this.''

Kate looked at the ad that Jessie shoved in front of her. A tall distinguished man in golfing clothes was posed on a golf course that looked like it was built on a hillside in the middle of a woods. "Come to the wilds and face the danger of the toughest course in America," the ad read. "Come to The Cabins.''

"A golf course?" She looked down at the bottom of the page. "In Kentucky?''

"Well, actually, there's a lot more stuff," Jessie said. "If you read on, it tells you about horseback riding and hiking trails and other outdoor stuff. There's even a lake. You could go skinny-dipping.''

Kate looked at her with contempt.

Jessie shrugged. "Okay, you couldn't, but somebody fun-loving and exciting could." She leaned forward. "But the real killer is the golf course—even I've heard of it. Executives pay a fortune to play it. It's like Outward Bound with martinis." She sat back and grinned at Kate. "Personally, I wouldn't be caught dead there, but I bet your Mr. Right is all over the place. Like shooting fish in a barrel.''

"Well, it does sound…interesting, I guess," Kate said, frowning at the ad. "But, I…''

"It's a goal and a plan," Jessie said. "You've gotten everything else you've ever wanted in life. You can get this, too."

"What makes you think I've gotten everything I've wanted?" Kate said, stung.

Jessie looked startled. "Well, you've..."

"If I have everything I want, why am I still running so hard?" Kate felt the resentment well up again. "Listen, I know I'm doing well—"

"Making four times your age with the same in blue chips," Jessie murmured.

"But I'm not happy. I want...I want a partnership with a man."

"A partnership is good," Jessie said, nodding. "Go for it."

Kate warmed to her fantasy, seeing herself beside that distinguished man, building an empire together while holding hands. "I want to work with my husband to build a business. I want..."

"A business!" Jessie was so disgusted she almost spat. "Forget business. Think relationship."

"I can't," Kate said. "Business is the only thing I know."

"Wrong." Jessie took a deep breath. "You're warm and loving. You take care of people. Or at least you used to." Jessie leaned over the table and grabbed Kate's arm. "You'd love to work with real people full-time, but the pay for working with people sucks, so you work with a bunch of suits instead and you go home alone. It's stupid, and you hate it." Jessie let go and then leaned back in her chair and sighed again. "I can't believe you've let money and success go to your head like this."

"Well, it's been lovely having breakfast with you," Kate said. "Leaving soon?"

Jessie took a deep breath. "Kate, please listen to me. Go to The Cabins, find a nice guy who's got all the things on your list and who can keep you with him forever, and be happy. All you have to do is choose to be happy. You can do it."

Jessie was so obviously concerned that Kate relented. "That's all," Kate said. "All I have to do is choose."

Jessie nodded once. "Yes."

Kate looked back down at the ad. Of course, the man in the picture was a model, but he was perfect. And she was due for a vacation before the summer was over, and since it was August she was definitely running out of summer. And she hadn't golfed in years.

And she was lonely. So lonely, sometimes she felt it in her bones.

"All right," she heard herself saying. "All right. I'll go."

"Yes!" Jessie pointed to Kate's French Provincial phone. "Go make your reservation now."

"I'll call later," Kate said. "Let me think about it for a while."

"No." Jessie folded her arms and leaned back in her chair. "I'm not leaving here until you call."

"I said I'm going," Kate said. "Don't you trust me?"

"No," Jessie said. "I'm keeping my eye on you on this one, because if anybody can screw up a perfectly good shot at happiness, you can. Call. *Now.*"

Two hundred miles away, Jake Templeton sat in an Adirondack chair on the back veranda of his brother's Kentucky resort with his feet propped on the rustic wooden rail, watching the sun rise over the lake and trying to feel content. Hell, he did feel content. There was the slight nagging feeling that he got sometimes that he might be missing something, but he was good at ignoring nagging—his long-ago marriage had taught him how to do that. And after all, he lived in God's country; he was free, he had no responsibilities aside from keeping a hundred acres of resort land mowed and watered, and no real worries. True, in the best of all possible worlds, his over-achieving younger brother would not have built a rustic resort on perfectly good farmland and would not have lured some of the biggest snobs in the East to play golf there. But the snobs did bring in a lot of money that kept the local population in food and shelter, and in general Jake didn't have to deal with them.

No. All in all, things were good. Jake pulled his big cream-colored cowboy hat down over his eyes and wallowed in his freedom. "I've got it made," he said out loud.

His brother backed out the door to join him carrying two steaming coffee mugs. Will was already in a suit, ready to meet his guests as they streamed in through the big carved-wood double doors of The Cabins. He looked at Jake in his tattered jeans and worn flannel shirt, and rolled his eyes; Jake looked up at his brother's dress-for-success tailoring and laughed.

"You're disgusting," Will said, looking down at him.

"What did I do now?" Jake asked, not caring.

"It's what you don't do." Will passed him a mug of coffee and sat down beside him to stare out at the lake.

"Hey, I keep this place looking good," Jake said, pushing his hat back with one hand while he balanced his mug in the other. He looked at his brother with a total lack of concern. "The grass is cut, the weeds are pulled, the golf courses look like artificial turf, the stables are—"

"I'm not talking about outdoor management," Will

said, shaking his head as he warmed his hands on his own coffee mug. "You are the king of the riding lawn mower. I'm talking about your life."

"I like my life. Stay out of it." Jake turned back to look at the lake and sipped the hot coffee carefully.

"You could be rich," Will said, looking at him with disgust.

"I was rich," Jake said. "Then I gave it all to you and you built this place." He shook his head. "That's the last fortune I give you."

"If you gave it to me, why do you own half of this place?" Will asked.

"So you'll be forced to support me in my old age," Jake said, grinning. "I'm not as dumb as I look."

Will shook his head again. "You've got a law degree. You were a tax attorney, for God's sake. And you gave it all up to mow lawns for your little brother. You should be ashamed."

"I don't actually mow the lawns," Jake pointed out. "I grab one of the college kids you hire for the season and say, 'Kid, mow that lawn.' It's not—"

"I don't understand why you quit," Will said.

"They bitched about my mustache, and they wouldn't let me wear my hat," Jake said. He looked back out over the lake and relaxed a little more. "Helluva sunrise, isn't it?"

"The sunrise was hours ago," Will said. "It's nine."

"Well, it's not all the way up yet," Jake said, slumping a little farther down in his chair. "So it's still rising. So it's still sunrise."

"Knock it off. I'm worried about you." Will frowned at him. "I think it's great that you're back home, and I couldn't run this place without you, but let's face it, you're wasting yourself here."

"I'm considering my options," Jake said lazily.

"You've been considering your options for five years," Will said bluntly. "And frankly, at the rate you're going, you don't have that many options to consider. It's time you made something of yourself again. One lousy marriage and you're down for the count."

Jake stared out at the lake and shook his head. "Boy, you sure don't see sunrises like this very often."

Will glared at him. "You see sunrises like this every damn day here."

"*I* do," Jake said, looking at him with equal disgust. "You don't. You're too busy being Mr. Hotel. If I'd known you were going to take this resort stuff so seriously, I would never have given you that money. Hell, you're going to have a heart attack any day now. Then I'll have to run this place."

"Well, somebody around here has to be an adult," Will said.

"And if you do croak on me, the first thing I'm going to do is blow up the golf courses."

"That'll piss Dad off."

"I think it's the clothes they wear that bother me the most," Jake began.

"We need to talk about this," Will said.

"No, we don't."

"Damn it, Jake…"

"Okay, okay. Get to the point. I'm missing a sunrise here."

Will shifted uneasily in his chair. "Look," he said finally. "You've always been my…well…?"

"Hero?" Jake suggested. "Idol?"

"Let's just stick with role model," Will said. "I spent my formative years trying to be just like you. It got to be a habit after a while." He looked over at his brother. "You were always the best. At everything."

"No, I wasn't," Jake said, irritated. "You just thought that because you were my younger brother."

"Jake, you haven't done anything for five years," Will said. "Nothing. Not since you moved back here to help me." Jake started to speak and Will cut him off. "I know, you run the outdoor staff. But hell, you could do that without getting out of bed. In fact, that's practically the way you do run it."

"Hey," Jake said.

"Listen, I need you here. You are a great help, and I will hate to see you go, but you've got to go back to the city."

"No," Jake said.

"You're not doing anything with your life," Will started, but this time Jake broke in.

"And that's the way I like it," Jake said. "Don't get the idea I'm sacrificing myself for you and this place. I'm not. I like it here. I'm staying."

Will tried another tack. "You ever think about getting married again?"

"No," Jake said. "Why are we talking about this?"

"Because if you were going to find anybody to marry in Toby's Corners, you would have married her by now," Will said. "This is another good reason to go back to the city."

"I'm not going back to the city," Jake said. "Now, will you please tell me what's going on?"

"Oh, hell." Will slumped down in his chair and rubbed his hand across his forehead.

"Just spit it out," Jake said, kindly. "You'll feel a lot better."

"Mom's worried about you," Will said. "And Valerie

thinks I'm taking advantage of you." He turned to face Jake. "You've really saved my life on this place. There are times when I look at the hell breaking loose inside the hotel and think, 'Thank God, Jake's got the outside under control.' I mean it. You make a big difference."

"I know," Jake said. "That's another reason I'm not leaving. But the main reason is because I don't want to." Jake sipped his coffee. "So Valerie's concerned for my welfare, huh?"

Will shot him a glance. "Yeah. I thought that was a little strange myself."

"I wondered when she was gonna make her move," Jake said.

Will raised his eyebrows. "Want to cut me in on this?"

"Valerie likes to think the hotel is a partnership deal."

"It is," Will said, confused. "You and me."

"No," Jake said. "You and her. I'm in the way."

"The way of what?" Will looked exasperated.

"The way of the two of you becoming the Leona and Harry Helmsley of the Midwest."

"God forbid," Will said. "You know, that woman is becoming a problem."

"Becoming?" Jake said. "I know she's sharing your apartment, which probably clouds your judgment. I know she's a great social director which, since you live and breathe this hotel, probably clouds your judgment even more, but she's also been a major pain in the butt ever since she got here."

"Yeah, well, I think that problem's about to be solved," Will said. "In the meantime, there's Mom. She's worried about you. And me," he added when Jake started to speak. "But mostly you. Because of your advanced age."

"Oh, hell," Jake said. "What's she want?"

"She wants us to get married. She wants grandkids."

Jake shrugged. "So, you give her some."

"I'm not married," Will said firmly. "And I'm not going to be."

Jake raised his eyebrows. "Valerie may have a different idea."

Will shook his head. "Valerie has plans for her future that do not include me, thank God." He sipped some coffee and thought before he went on. "One of those big chains has been scouting her. They're going to be offering her big bucks any day now to be social director of the East Coast or something, and she will be gone."

Jake looked at his brother curiously. "And you're not concerned about this?"

"I'm relieved. Valerie really is a terrific woman, and I appreciate everything she's done for the resort, but she's getting on my nerves. You know, I'm not even sure how we ended up living together."

"I am," Jake said, turning back to the lake. "Sex. It's a powerful force, my boy, and women use it."

"Is that why you gave them up?" Will asked, sympathetically. "Did paranoia drive you to celibacy?"

"It's not paranoia if they really are out to get you," Jake said. "And frankly, I think Valerie's got you. And I'll bet Valerie thinks so, too."

"Nobody's got me," Will said. "I'm married to my job."

Jake looked at him as if he were demented.

"Hey, some of us have careers," Will protested. "Besides, I'm not ready for anything serious."

"Three years sharing a hotel suite isn't serious?"

"See, this is the kind of stuff I get from Mom." Will narrowed his eyes at his brother. "Which brings me back to my point. I think Valerie and Mom are right."

"I hate this," Jake said. "You feel guilty, so I get to suffer."

"You need some focus to your life, some goals, something to look forward to besides a sunrise." Will looked stern. "If you don't want to move back to the city, fine. But I think you should get married."

"I did," Jake said, looking back at the lake. "I didn't like it. It's your turn to screw up your life. I did mine already."

"So you're happy in your lonely little cabin at the end of that lonely little lane," Will said. "All by yourself in that big cold bed."

"Don't ever go into psychology," Jake said. "You have the subtlety of a rock."

"Don't you ever think about the perfect woman?" Will said.

"Sure," Jake said. "She's about five foot two, somewhere between eighteen and twenty, dumb as a coot, and she thinks I'm God."

Will looked disgusted. "She'd have to be dumb as a coot to pull that last one off. I'm serious, here."

"The thing about women," Jake said, "is that they got liberated too fast. They never learned to be straightforward about life because they had to sneak around for about a thousand years tricking men into doing things they wanted. So they manipulate you instead of telling you what they want, so you never know where the hell you are. And then they get mad at you and bitch." He swallowed a mouthful of coffee and shook his head. "I have had it up to here with smart-mouthed, overly brainy, manipulative women."

"So don't get married to Tiffany again," Will said reasonably. "Find your moronic midget and marry her. And then get your life moving before you turn into a potted plant and the help starts watering you."

Jake ignored him and went on. "If I ever do hook up with anybody again—and I sincerely doubt that I will, so wipe that hopeful look off your face—it will be with someone who thinks that being with somebody who mows lawns is her idea of heaven on earth and who will do exactly what I tell her to do and love it."

"I think Donna Reed is dead," Will said.

Jake slid down farther in his chair. "Well, then, I'm not getting married again. Over to you, bro."

"Now wait a minute," Will began, but he stopped when he heard the reservations phone ringing inside the office.

"Another sucker who wants to pay too much money to play vertical golf." Jake shook his head. "I thought you were nuts when you had that course built on the hillside, but they do come running."

The phone rang again.

"Concentrate on getting married and resuming your regularly scheduled life," Will said on his way back inside. "Who knows? Maybe this is your future bride calling right now."

"Like hell," Jake said and went back to the sunrise.

Two

Kate didn't notice how lovely the little town was until she'd driven halfway through it. The four-hour drive down to the resort had been filled with thoughts of dread, panic, and the fancy underwear that Jessie had talked her into buying as inspiration. She was still trying to decide whether the best plan was to do a dignified sulk for the next two weeks or to wear the underwear and develop a better attitude, when she realized how charming everything around her was.

The shady old streets were lined with thick-trunked trees and the antique storefronts were painted in faded roses and blues and yellows with gold-edged lettering in the windows. Cline's Dry Goods. Dickerson's Snack Shop. Beamis Hardware. Stores with family names that had probably been there for generations. The whole town of Toby's Corners smelled of dust and honeysuckle, and Kate drove through it all and thought of Mary Jane shoes and ice-cream cones and football games and all the things she'd read about but never known.

This would have been a lovely place to grow up, she thought. *This would have felt like a home. Maybe my life would have been different if I'd started out in a place like Toby's Corners—a place full of dusty sunlight and trees and possibilities.*

And then she shook her head. *Pull yourself together,*

Kate, she told herself. *You have a goal and a plan. Concentrate.*

She turned right at a low slung white building that said *Nancy's Place* in pink neon over the double wood doors and slowed to look at it. It had to be a bar or a restaurant—the parking lot was the biggest she'd seen in the town so far—but it was the most low-key bar she'd ever seen, no signs for beer or ads for Wet-T-shirt Wednesdays, just an anciet handpainted "Welcome" sign in white on the knotty-pine doors. Even the bars in this town were clean and cute. She'd landed in Disneyland Kentucky.

Past *Nancy's Place,* the road began to wind into the woods. The subtle light felt cool, almost sensuous as she drove slowly under the trees, savoring the woodsy smell. The woods were dim and secret, and when she shivered, it wasn't just from the chill of leaving the sun. *There's something...exciting about the woods,* she thought. *Maybe something will happen here. Maybe I'll fall in love. Maybe everything will work out here. Jessie said all I have to do is choose. Well, I choose to be happy and successful and...and unafraid. I'll be like Jessie. Absolutely fearless. I'll even get up early tomorrow and find the lake, and I'll swim in the nude. I really will.*

Then she rounded the last turn, and thought, *Oh, maybe not.*

The resort stood before her looking like a log cabin with a thyroid problem. Much larger than it had seemed in the brochure, it rose up in ranks of clustered cabins, carefully stacked like children's blocks at slight angles to one another, each with a private natural-wood deck. Abraham Lincoln's place crossed with Tara, midwifed by Frank Lloyd Wright.

Oh, no, Kate thought. *It's too big.*

Even worse, there seemed to be at least a thousand people milling around. If she went skinny-dipping in the morning, she'd probably turn up in vacation slides all over the Midwest—"And here's a shot of that crazy woman who used to go swimming buck naked every morning. Notice how her breasts are startin' to droop?"

She sighed and pulled up next to the hotel entrance.

I hate this! Kate thought. She steeled herself and walked through the big carved double doors into the lobby, looking cool and efficient in her silk suit, detached from everyone around her. One of the generic distinguished-looking men Jessie had promised her held the door for her as she went in, but she was concentrating so hard on maintaining her image that she noticed him as a possibility only in passing. Later. One thing at a time. Where had all these people come from?

The desk manager smiled at her as she signed the register card. "Welcome to The Cabins, Miss Swanson."

"Svenson."

"Of course. I'm Will Templeton. We're really glad you're here."

Kate repressed the impulse to ask why. Will Templeton was tall, dark, and ruggedly handsome, and he was glad to see her. It would take a woman with an extremely bad attitude to assume that what this man was truly glad to see was her Visa card.

"You'll want to see my Visa card," Kate said.

"No, no, that was all taken care of when you reserved by phone. You're in cabin 9A. Up past the tennis courts there and beyond the croquet lawn. You can park your car right behind the cabin."

The croquet lawn. Well, it could be worse. They'd have to stop knocking balls around when the sun went down. And at least she wasn't staying in that rabbit warren of a hotel with God-knows-who....

From behind her, a lilting soprano bubbled, "Was that cabin 9A, you said?"

The manager said, "I certainly did, Miss Craft," and Kate turned.

Miss Craft, young, blond, and built like a Barbie doll, had eyes of cornflower blue, a tilted-up nose, and a genuinely sweet smile on her lovely full lips. She looked about nineteen.

Great, Kate thought. *My competition. I bet nothing on her droops. I bet she doesn't even wear underwear.*

"I'm Penny Craft," the Barbie doll said, holding out her hand to Kate. "I'll be right next door in 9B."

"Oh, good," Kate said.

"And I was wondering, if you'd mind, could you possibly give me a lift to the cabin? With my luggage? The bellboys here are real busy...."

"No problem," Kate said. "I'd be happy to." She took her key from Will and tried hard to ignore him when he called after them. "Don't you ladies forget the luau tonight."

"Oh, we sure won't," Penny Craft squealed back.

Luggage said a lot about a person, Kate realized as she walked Penny to the car. She herself had one charcoal-gray suitcase and a briefcase. Penny had three pieces of pink luggage. *Guess which one of us has more fun,* Kate thought as she helped Penny load her bags into the car. Then she began the drive to the cabin, going slowly to avoid all the people who dodged in front of her on the way, evidently having such a good time that they wanted to die where they stood.

Kate glared at one of them. "This place has too many people."

"Oh, no." Penny waved to someone. "I *love* people."

"I sensed that."

Penny smiled at her. "They say it's a lot quieter near the cabins."

Kate looked at her curiously. "I'd think you'd prefer the hotel."

"No." Penny waved to someone else. "I'm planning on seeing all the guys I can while I'm here, and you know how nosy people in hotels are."

"What do you mean, 'seeing'?"

"Oh, you know—dance, talk, laugh... Have as much fun as possible," Penny said cheerfully. "I'm getting married next month. This is my last chance."

"Oh," Kate said after a pause. "Well, good luck."

"Thank you." Penny turned and looked at her. "Why did you come here?"

Good question. She was going to strangle Jessie. "Oh, you know—to dance, talk, laugh." Kate glared at all the people swarming around her car. "Maybe swim naked in the pool."

"Are you allowed to do that?"

Kate closed her eyes. Penny really was as dumb as a rock. "If you get up very early," she said.

"Oh. I thought maybe you were writing a travel article or something."

"A travel article? Why?"

"Well, why else would somebody all businesslike like you be up here?"

"To meet men?" Kate suggested.

"Oh, sure," Penny said and giggled.

* * *

Cabin 9, when they found it after two wrong turns, was several yards from the croquet field, and Kate cheered up when she saw how private it was. She was even happier when she took her briefcase inside. The bedroom, paneled in knotty pine, was compact but cozy, and Kate dropped her briefcase on the patchwork-covered double bed with a sigh of relief. This was going to be fine. She needed a rest, and this was lovely. Even if she didn't meet anyone...

She stopped. Of course, she was going to meet someone. She had a plan. She squared her shoulders and went outside to unload the luggage.

Kate was putting the last of Penny's suitcases on the ground when a man strolled down the path with his hands in his pockets.

"Need any help?" he asked lazily as he came near her, and she was forced to turn and look at him. He was big, broad, and slow-moving, dressed in plaid flannel and denim. His hair was thick, dark and untrimmed, his black-brown eyes were lazy, and his nose had definitely been broken at least once in the past; it lurched slightly to the left over his full, neat mustache. But the finishing touch for Kate was his generous, cream-colored Stetson hat.

A cowboy hat. Unbelievable.

Then he smiled at her—a friendly, no-come-on smile—and she almost smiled back before she caught herself. *Absolutely not,* she told herself. *You are not going to fall for some dumb, macho, good-looking good old boy. You have a plan. He is not part of your plan. Besides, he looks like a cowboy, and you're not interested in cowboys. Especially not this far north of the Rio Grande.*

"I think I can manage." She turned to pull her suitcase out of the car. "Thank you."

"Well, *hello.*" They both turned at the sound of Penny's voice to see her standing at the top of the porch steps, slender and lovely, vibrating with pleasure at seeing a man.

"Penny, this is…?" Kate faced him.

"Jake." He touched his hat to Penny.

"Jake, this is Penny," Kate said. "Jake has offered to help with the luggage."

"Well, you sweet thing, you," Penny cooed. "I'd adore your help. Mine's the pink stuff down there."

"Coming right up," Jake said, and he bent to pick up all of Penny's remaining pieces of luggage.

"You must be so strong." Penny beamed at him.

"Nope. Just too lazy to make two trips." He ambled up the steps to the porch.

Well, there's the start of a beautiful relationship, Kate thought, and took her suitcase into the cabin.

A few minutes later, Jake went down the path shaking his head. All those macho guys who said women were all alike had never met Penny Craft and Kate Svenson. When he'd first seen the two trim blondes from a couple of hundred yards down the path, he'd assumed they were sisters. On a closer look, he'd decided they couldn't possibly belong to the same family. Now, after spending five minutes with them, he wasn't sure they belonged on the same planet.

Penny was every young man's dream—cute, friendly and undemanding. Being nice to Penny would be no hardship, although listening to her babble for more than fifteen minutes might test a man's patience. He grinned. Probably only his patience; any other man would listen to her if she spoke Swahili, as long as he could look at her. He must be getting old. Penny was a dream come true, all right, but she was someone else's dream, not his.

If Penny was somebody else's dream, Kate was his own personal nightmare. Who the hell would come to the country wearing a silk suit? And she had her blond hair yanked back so hard in that twist that her eyebrows slanted. He remembered the way she'd looked at him as he'd walked toward her—sizing him up and then dismissing him with those icy blue eyes. "Thank you," she'd said and walked away. The temperature must have dropped ten degrees around her cabin.

He shuddered. Kate reminded him of Valerie and his ex-wife, Tiffany. Women like that always got what they wanted no matter what it took, not caring who they trampled on to get their way. Efficient. Calculating. Manipulative. Most likely she'd come to the resort to sharpen her golf game, get a tan, snare a husband, and improve her stock portfolio. *God preserve me from a woman like that*, he thought, and grinned again. God wouldn't have to preserve him from a woman like Kate Svenson. She'd made it very clear that she wasn't interested.

Forget her, he told himself, and wandered down the path to troubleshoot the luau.

Penny came to pick Kate up for the luau at six, and Kate steeled herself for the ordeal ahead. *This is the only way you're going to meet men*, she told herself. *Jessie's right. Just relax and have a good time. Stop whining. Be a woman.*

Penny had dressed by wrapping a turquoise flowered sarong over a tiny yellow bikini. Her earrings were turquoise, with yellow parrots on swings—the parrots made of real feathers. She was too much of everything, and yet, in her obvious happiness, she was just right.

I could never wear an outfit like that, Kate reflected. *Not unless I was very, very drunk.* She was feeling very, very superior until a traitorous little voice inside her added, *Maybe that's why I don't have any fun.*

"Put on your bathing suit," Penny said to Kate. "Maybe we'll get thrown in the pool."

"We can only hope," Kate said. Her bathing suit was an old black one-piece, years out of style but hardly worn. She put on white slacks and a white shirt over it, tying the shirttails in a knot on her stomach.

"That's it?" Penny asked.

"That's it."

"That's kind of plain," Penny said.

"That's the kind of woman I am," Kate said. "Plain. Let's go."

Penny hesitated, frowning. "Don't you want to let your hair down or something? I mean, this is a *luau.*"

"No," Kate said evenly. "I like it up."

"Well, you don't look very relaxed."

"This is as relaxed as I get," she said.

"Okay," Penny said, shaking her head. "Maybe you'll feel better after a couple of drinks."

"Don't count on it," Kate said.

The luau, when they got there, was everything she'd feared and more.

The grounds around the hotel were packed with people in various stages of excitement and inebriation, dressed in various interpretations of what the well-dressed vacationer should wear to a luau. Hawaiian shirts dominated, but there was also a healthy contingent of sarongs and one grass skirt. The guy in the grass skirt didn't have the legs for it.

People clustered at round redwood tables, laughing uproariously at each other's jokes. Small children ran by, shrieking, chasing each other with pineapple-punch drinks. Overfriendly couples danced badly to the Beach Boys. A huge dead animal was turning on a spit as people lined up to accept chunks of its overcooked flesh. The air smelled of suntan lotion and burned meat.

"Isn't this terrific?" Penny glowed with excitement.

Kate looked around, horrified. "Where did all these people come from? They can't be all from the hotel."

"They come from all around." Penny waved to someone. "The hotel does this every month during the summer on the third Saturday night. Isn't it great? See the tall guy with the dark hair over there beside the pig roast?"

"That's a pig?"

"That's Will. Remember? From the desk? I thought he was just a clerk, but he's the owner. I think he's dishy."

"Go for it," Kate said, looking around for a bar. There had to be one. People couldn't be behaving this badly without alcohol.

"The dark guy in the red shirt is Eric Allingham. He's loaded." Penny waved to someone else. "Money all over the place."

"Go for it." There had to be a bar somewhere.

"He's not my type."

"You're not interested in money?"

"Why would I be interested in money?" Penny asked. "I'm getting married."

Kate was startled, but when she considered it, Penny made sense, if you accepted the basic proposition that dating around a month before you got married was a sound idea.

"Sorry." Kate shook her head. "I wasn't thinking."

"The blond guy in the Izod shirt is cute, though. His name is Lance something."

"How did you learn all this?"

"Oh, I sat in the lobby and talked to people while I was waiting for the bellboy. People here are really friendly."

"Great," Kate said. "I don't suppose you know where they put the bar for this event?"

"It's out by the pool."

"Lead me there."

The pool was inside a high-hedged enclosure. Tiled in blue and white, it reflected the Japanese lanterns strung overhead. The bar, a long counter trimmed with grass matting, was presided over by an efficient red-haired college-age boy in a white shirt and a pink lei. He looked as if he could have done without the lei. His bar was doing a brisk business in middle-aged men who welcomed Penny as if she were a large dry martini. Penny was surrounded, and Kate waited for a turn at the bar for both of them.

"What'll it be, ma'am?"

"Penny." Kate reached out her hand and hauled her into the crush. "Meet the bartender. What's your name?"

"Mark." The bartender smiled broadly at Penny.

"This is Penny, Mark," Kate said. "I'll have a double Scotch. She'll let you know what she wants."

"She can have anything I've got," Mark said.

"You sweet thing," Penny said.

The start of another beautiful relationship. Kate shook her head. *I may have to take lessons from this girl.*

She took her drink and wandered over to the pool where she rolled up her pant legs and sat on the edge, dangling her feet in the water, sipping her drink, and inhaling the chlorine along with the cool evening air. *I have such a bad attitude,* she thought. *Probably because, unlike Penny, I really don't want to do this. I don't want to be alone anymore, but I don't want to go out and cold-bloodedly look for a man, either. What I really want is the fairy tale where Prince Charming just appears out of nowhere and sweeps me off my feet and takes me… where? To his condominium, conveniently located close to his thriving business? So much for romance, Kate.*

She was laughing quietly at herself when a man appeared out of nowhere and sat down on the other side of her. He was balding, overweight and overdrunk, and he was wearing six leis.

"Hello, pretty lady sitting here all alone."

"Hello," Kate said, edging away.

"I'm Frank," he said, putting his arm around her.

"And Earnest, too, I imagine," she said, removing his arm.

Out of the corner of her eye, she saw Mark signal to someone outside the enclosure.

"I've been looking all over for you, honey."

"Why?" Kate asked. "Have we met?"

"Only in my dreams."

"Get new dreams."

Kate stood, trying to gently but firmly push him away as she did, but Frank grabbed her hand and got up, too. It took him a while, and Kate would have wandered politely away during the struggle but he held on to her with fingers of steel until he finally lunged nose-to-nose with her.

"Do you know what you need?" he breathed. "You need a lei." He laughed uproariously. "A lay. Get it?"

He tried to take off one of his leis and almost strangled himself.

"No." Kate pulled her hand from his and turned to walk away. "I'm not interested in a lei."

"You're not saying no to me, are you?" Frank asked roguishly, catching her arm.

"Over and over again," Kate assured him, trying to pry his fingers off her.

"Good." He pulled her closer. "I love a feisty woman."

Kate turned eyes like razors on him.

Jake saw Mark's wave and came into the enclosure in time to see Frank pulling drunkenly on Kate.

Oh, great. Now he'd have her complaining to Will about the quality of the guests. He watched her try to fend Frank off and admitted to himself that she'd have a point if she did. He sighed and moved up behind them in time to hear Frank take her arm and say, "I love a feisty woman."

"How would you like to be a soprano?" Kate asked him, and Jake intervened.

"How's it going, Frank?" Jake clapped him on the shoulder and yanked him away from Kate.

"Jake, old buddy." Frank leaned into him. "I should have known if there was a good-looking woman around, you'd be there." He attempted to punch Jake on the shoulder and missed him by a good inch. Jake turned him gently around toward the pig roast.

"Lots of pretty women out there, Frank."

"Sorry, Jake. Didn't know this one was yours." Frank wiggled his fingers at Kate and ambled off while they watched him.

"Thank you," Kate said. "You're a very tactful bouncer."

"Well, we aim to please," Jake said. "Besides, I was afraid you were going to hurt him."

"That was my plan," Kate said. "Your way was better." She smiled up at him gratefully, and Jake was startled by how human she looked. A little too human. He stepped back, but she'd turned away and was watching Frank stagger out of the enclosure.

"You know, as glad as I am to see him go, this is the story of my life," Kate said. "Men leaving me."

"Frank will come back if I yell," Jake offered.

"No, no." Kate shook her head bravely. "I'll just sit here and nurse my broken heart. And what's left of my Scotch."

"Kate," Penny called to her. "Come meet these dishy guys."

"Now there. Isn't that nice?" Jake grinned at her.

"Peachy," she said. "I love dishy guys."

He watched her join Penny and the two upwardly mobile jerks she'd found. Penny might be cute, but she had no discrimination when it came to men. Kate, he'd be willing to bet, had too much discrimination. Nobody would be good enough for her. She'd have to find somebody who was close to what she wanted and change him, improve him by slashing at him with those eyes, trying to wind him around her little finger....

Jake shook his head to get rid of the image. Kate was not his problem. The luau, however, was, so he sighed and went to see what else was going wrong.

Propelled back into the middle of the luau, Kate found herself introduced to Penny's dishy guys, Chad and Lance, partners in an Ohio real-estate agency. Actually, as Kate tried to convince herself a few minutes later, there was nothing really wrong with Chad and Lance. They were overly hearty and overly macho, and Lance did have a tendency to drape his arm around her and send her meaningful glances and—Kate was mentally crossing him off when she stopped herself. *This is what you came for,* she told herself. *Be nice to Lance. Get to know him. Maybe this Andrew Dice Idiot attitude he's wearing is merely to cover up his insecurity and vulnerability. Maybe he simply needs someone to understand him. Be nice to him.*

In fact, she vowed, *I'm going to be nice to everyone, and stop being such a snob.*

She gave it her best shot, agreeing to have dinner with Lance later, valiantly attempting to be at least half as enthusiastic toward him as Penny was with Chad. Still, after half an hour of evading Lance's hands, Kate had reached the end of her patience.

"I'll be right back," she said, smiling at him.

"I'll come with you," Lance said reaching for her again.

"No, really." Kate backed off, waving her glass. Then she wheeled around and lost herself in the crowd, stopping only when an efficient-looking blonde caught at her hand.

"You're Kate Svenson," she said, shaking Kate's captured hand. "I'm Valerie Borden, the social director here."

"Oh. Hello, Ms. Border," Kate said, still checking over her shoulder for Lance.

"Borden. But you must call me Valerie. We're all friends here at The Cabins."

Wonderful. Kate turned to look at Valerie for the first time.

Valerie was tall, blond, polished, and patrician. Kate felt as if she were looking into a mirror except that Valerie was smiling.

"We're so glad you're here, Kate," Valerie said. "I'd love to sit and talk with you some time. I'm sure we have so much in common."

"We do?" Kate said.

"Absolutely. But it's time to party now. We don't want you to be alone." Valerie tucked Kate's hand under her arm and led her into the crowd near the pool. "Let me introduce you to some people. Is there anyone in particular you'd like to meet?"

Kate looked at her trapped hand and decided to play along. Resisting Valerie was bound be exhausting and fruitless anyway; Valerie was plainly a woman who routinely got what she wanted. "Tall, distinguished, rich businessmen," Kate said, remembering Jessie and the wish list. "It's an assignment."

Valerie blinked at her bluntness and then recovered. "All right," she said and proceeded to make good her word.

Kate debated the state of the environment with Rick, who was tall, distinguished and the head of his own ecological impact firm. She learned about polo ponies from Eric, who was tall, distinguished and the VP of a consulting firm. She discussed the market with Donald, who was tall, distinguished and vague about what he did for a living. She agreed that golf was the only civilized game with Peter, who was tall, distinguished and the owner of a public relations firm, and who persuaded her to play golf with him the next afternoon. And eventually, she found herself back with tall, sort-of-distinguished Lance, the real-estate agent. Unfortunately, Lance, after several drinks, was even more of a trial than he'd been earlier.

Lance was starting to run to fat, but his face was still handsome despite the fact that his eyes were a little too small and a little too mean. He was also a big guy and he liked using his size. He muscled them a place in line until Kate said, "Oh, let's go back to the end. It's quieter there." He also had hands. He stood behind her as they got in line for the burned pig, standing too close. He put his hand on her shoulder. He put his hand on her arm. He put his hand on her waist. When he moved his hand again, she put a plate in it.

"Could you take this for me?" she asked him. "I'll bring the drinks."

They ate with Penny and Chad at one of the ubiquitous round redwood tables, and the night passed slowly—excruciatingly slowly—while people whooped and screeched around them.

Lance said something and Penny laughed, so Kate laughed, too, only a beat behind. Lance didn't seem to mind.

"Lance, you're such a riot," Penny said. "Don't you think so, Kate?"

"Absolutely. Anyone for another Scotch?" She toddled back to the bar by the pool before any of them could join her.

"Hello, Mark," she said, leaning on the bar.

"Hello, Kate," the bartender said, laughing. "How's it going?"

"Don't ask."

Mark leaned forward a little. "What are you doing with that Lance creep, anyway? He's trouble."

"It's a long story. How about another Scotch?"

"You sure?"

"Kate, honey," Lance said from behind her. "I couldn't find you anywhere."

"I'm sure," Kate said to Mark, and he shook his head and poured.

Kate took her Scotch and wandered over by the pool, and Lance followed her, hands outstretched. Out of the corner of her eye, she saw Mark motion to someone outside the pool. Why did he do that? she wondered, and then concentrated on handling Lance. She listened to him for a while, skillfully evading his hands, but finally gave up. It was no use. She could drink enough Scotch to fill the pool, and she still wouldn't marry Lance.

She poured her Scotch into the pool.

"What are you doing?"

"Sobering up."

"Oh, don't do that, honey." He put his hand on her rear end.

"Move your hand, Lance."

He moved it around to her breast. "Come on, baby."

"Better men than you have lost arms that way, Lance," she said, moving his hand.

"I want you, Kate." He reached around and squeezed her rear end.

"I don't want you, Lance," she said and pushed him into the pool.

"I wish you hadn't done that," Jake said from behind her.

"Where'd you come from?" Kate asked, watching Lance try to find the surface.

"Mark calls me if there's trouble. That's twice tonight he's been a little worried about you. First Frank, now Lance."

"Mark's very sweet."

"We both really enjoyed watching you with Lance."

"Speaking of Lance, is he going to drown?"

"Give him a chance," Jake said. "He'll find the way up pretty soon."

"And if he doesn't?"

"Then I'll help him." Jake eased himself down until he was sitting on his heels by the pool. "See, here he comes."

Lance broke sputtering through the surface of the water, and Jake reached down and caught him. When Lance caught his breath, he looked at Kate. "You lousy bi—"

Jake pushed his head back under the water for a minute and then hauled him up by his collar.

"Sorry, Lance. My hand slipped." He pulled him dripping from the pool. Lance gagged, and Jake let him go and pounded him on the back.

"Well, it's been a lovely evening, but I really must go." Kate smiled at Jake. "Thank you again. Good night." She waved to Mark and strolled out of the pool enclosure.

"I don't think she's your type, Lance," she heard Jake say. "She doesn't seem to appreciate a great guy like you."

Jake helped Lance into the hotel and put him on the elevator to his room. Lance's main topic of conversation was Kate, and he wasn't flattering. "I hope that frozen bitch burns" was the last thing he said as the elevator doors closed.

Surprising himself, Jake disagreed. Yeah, she was frozen, but you had to admire a woman who could take care of a creep like Lance so neatly. She'd put him in the pool with one quick push and then stood calmly on the side waiting for him to come up. There was a lot to be said for a woman who could take care of herself. Then he stopped himself. Cool, efficient, independent. Those were the qualities he'd fallen for in a woman once before, and she'd turned out to be a chilly, expensive mistake. The same mistake his brother was about to make with Valerie. *Don't be dumb, Jake,* he warned himself, and went back to the luau.

The light from the ginger-jar lamps on each side of the big bed filled the room with a soft glow. The room felt homey and warm, and Kate relaxed once her door was closed behind her.

Lance was just a mistake, she decided as she got ready for bed. Tomorrow she would do better. Tomorrow she would play golf with and fall in love with Peter, the public relations ace, and they would live successfully ever after, playing upscale golf in their free time.

For some reason, that prospect did not appeal to her and she fell asleep feeling vaguely uneasy about her own plan for the future. That unease followed her into her dreams, plaguing her with visions of overweight blond men trying to snare her with leis while she searched for somebody else—somebody she couldn't remember when she woke up the next morning. *I'm not even cooperating in my dreams,* she thought as she climbed out of bed. *Get back to your plan, Kate. Work on it.*

The problem was that she hated her plan even more in the daylight than she had the night before. She wanted to be swept off her feet. She wanted to see him across a crowded room and love him so much and want him so much that she wouldn't be able to stand it. Love at first sight. Love that would last forever.

Fat chance. She argued herself back to her game plan. After all, what she was looking for wasn't love at first sight, anyway, because that kind of love didn't last. No, she wanted a practical love, partnering a distinguished successful man; the kind of love that two people of similar backgrounds carefully and thoughtfully constructed for themselves. That was reality.

Get a grip on your life, woman! she thought. *Make it happen. Go out and meet people this morning, have a nice lunch, and then play golf with Peter this afternoon. Something will happen. You can do it. Jessie said so.*

She put on some of the new lacy underwear Jessie had picked out for her, and then covered it sensibly with beige shorts and a white sleeveless blouse. Her chignon looked a little formal with the shorts, so she just pulled her hair back and wound it into a loose knot. When she left the cabin, the sky was the clear, bright, vivid blue that only happens in August. The heat was building, but the breeze was cool and the trees were full of birds singing their heads off. She was pleased with herself and with the beautiful day, and she hummed as she strolled up to the hotel for a late nine o'clock breakfast.

Then Valerie caught her.

"We're going to do wonderful things today," Valerie told her, drawing her into a group of other late risers. The hotel as represented by Valerie obviously wanted its guests involved in life. Although that had been Kate's sincere plan, when suddenly confronted with the reality of mingling with others, she backed off, appalled.

"Not right now, Valerie," she said, trying to sidle off.

"Tennis, croquet, golf, horseback riding, or tag in the pool—what's it going to be?" Valerie drew her inexorably back into the group.

I'd rather die, Kate thought.

"What's it going to be, Kathy, honey?" Frank was in front of her, dressed in a wide-striped T-shirt, bouncing on his heels. "How about pool tag?" He leered at her. "I want to see you in that bathing suit."

"I don't think so." Kate backed away again. "Thanks."

She turned and saw Jake, walking down the drive, carrying fishing poles, a small six-pack cooler, and a duffel bag of what looked to be cushions. He was wearing cutoffs that had seen much better days, an old, torn, checked shirt, and his cowboy hat. He nodded briefly at her and walked past her toward the woods, his hat tilted down to keep the sun off his face.

"Well, you have to do something," Valerie said with a determined smile. "You can't just sit."

"I am doing something." Kate jerked her thumb at Jake. "I'm going fishing with Jake." She turned and walked down the path behind him, taking long strides to catch up.

"You don't actually have to take me fishing," she told him, knowing he'd heard. "Just let me stay with you until we're into the woods and I'm safe."

He didn't say anything for a minute, and then handed her the poles without looking at her or breaking his slow, relaxed amble. "There's an extra pole and room in the boat."

Kate hesitated a moment, but when she looked back, Valerie was watching her.

And I'm paying a lot of money for this, she thought. *I'm going to kill Jessie.* Then she sighed and turned to follow Jake through the woods to the lake.

Three

The lake was small, secluded, and green. Pulled up on its stony shore was a wide shallow rowboat that looked like it had lost its paint before Kate had been born.

"This floats?"

"Oh, yeah." Jake tossed the duffel in. "I wouldn't jump up and down in it, but it floats."

"There aren't any seats," Kate said.

"Somebody ripped them out once to use as oars." Jake pushed the boat most of the way into the water. "Stack the cushions. If you're still coming."

Kate looked over her shoulder. Valerie was definitely out of sight, but she was also one of the most determined women Kate had ever met. Better to take no chances. She stepped carefully into the boat and dumped the duffel out. There were half a dozen square blue plastic-covered boat cushions, and several faded-pink sofa pillows. She stacked three of the plastic cushions at each end and sat on one stack, her hands neatly folded in front of her. Jake climbed in opposite her and pushed off, rowing when the boat had floated a little way into the lake. It was the most energetic thing she'd seen him do, but even here he was lazy, rowing with long, slow strokes. She watched his hands on the oars and the flex of the muscles in his forearms, mesmerized by the slow movement of his body as he pulled the oars deeply through the water.

He rowed them into the shade of a willow on the far bank, tied the boat to an overhanging branch, and spread the plastic cushions he'd been sitting on behind him, topping them with the sofa pillows. Kate did the same with her cushions and leaned back to watch him.

Every move he made was slow, she realized, but exactly efficient. He picked up his rod, cast his line expertly into the water, and then jammed the pole between the gunwale of the boat and the oarlock. No wasted movement. While she was still admiring his efficiency, he kicked off his shoes and took off his shirt.

His shoulders were broad, with the kind of muscle that came from everyday work. He leaned toward her and she tensed, remembering Lance, but all he did was hand her the second rod. "Beer's in the cooler," he said, and settled back into the cushions at his end of the boat, the pillows under his head, tipping his hat over his face until all she could see was the curve of his mouth under his mustache.

Kate looked at her rod.

"Jake," she said softly. "There's no bait on my hook."

"If you bait your hook," he said patiently from under his hat, "you will catch a fish."

She waited for further explanation but he was finished. Evidently for Jake, fishing meant sleeping half naked under a willow tree. When she thought about it, it made sense. She didn't like fish anyway.

She cast her line in and jammed her pole beside his and then made herself a nest in the cushions, stretching her legs out beside his, careful not to touch him. She leaned back and stared up through the willow, listening to the water lap the side of the boat and the wind gently stir the drooping silver leaves above her. The sound was narcotic, and after a while Kate began to relax for the first time in as long as she could remember. *Maybe life doesn't count out here,* she thought lazily. *Maybe time stops out here, and nothing matters. Maybe it's magic.* She smiled and watched the clouds, filtered through the curtain of willow leaves above her.

After a while she looked over at Jake. His chest was rising and falling in slow deep rhythms, and unconsciously she started to breathe with him, feeling the last of the tension drain from her body as the boat drifted gently in the water.

It was a shame he wasn't her type. He wasn't bad-looking, even with the broken nose, and he was certainly the most restful man she'd ever met. But he definitely did not fit her plan. He didn't have a distinguished or aggressive bone in his body. In fact, looking at him now, she wasn't sure he had bones in his body. He just sort of flowed everywhere. He'd get eaten alive in the city.

Still, it was nice to relax with a man for a change. Even if he was unconscious.

Her line jerked.

She sat up and grasped the pole, catching the reel as it played out. There was definitely something tugging on the other end.

"Jake," she said softly. He didn't move, and she could tell by his even breathing that he was still asleep. "Jake," she said louder, but he slept on.

The fish jerked against her line. "Jake!" she yelled, smacking him on the leg with her foot.

The breathing stopped. "What?" he said, from under his hat.

"I've got a fish."

"That's nice."

"I don't want it."

"Throw it back."

"Jake."

He yawned and sat up slowly, pushing his hat back on his head. "If I'd known you were going to be this energetic, I wouldn't have brought you."

"I didn't do this on purpose." She reeled her line in and a tiny sunfish broke the water.

"You got an aquarium?" Jake asked.

She brought the pole around to grab the fish, but it flipped and struggled and she couldn't catch it. After it had flipped past his face twice, Jake reached up and caught it, easing the hook out of its mouth and tossing it back in the water.

"Thank you," she said.

"You're welcome."

"Do you have a knife?"

"Depends on what you want to use it for."

"To cut this damn hook off before any more fish try to commit suicide on my line."

He grinned at her and gave her his pocketknife. She cut the line above the hook and handed both the hook and the knife back to him. Then she dropped her line in the water and leaned back in the boat. "Thank you," she said. "Sorry to have bothered you."

"Not at all." He started to lean back and stopped. "Do you have to be back by any certain time?"

"I'm playing golf at two with Peter somebody," Kate said. "If I set foot on shore much before that, Valerie will make me play with the other kids. I am in no hurry, trust me."

"Valerie is nobody to mess with," Jake agreed. "So you're playing vertical golf, are you?"

"What? On that hill? Absolutely not," Kate said.

"We're playing on the wimp course in back of the hotel."

"Want to bet?" Jake said.

"Do you know something I don't?"

"If this is the Peter I'm thinking about, he cheats," Jake said. "And it's a lot easier to cheat on the hard course."

"He doesn't cheat," Kate said, looking at Jake with disgust. "Just look at him. He has 'man of distinction' written all over him, just like in one of those expensive liquor ads."

"Those are usually the ones who cheat," Jake said. "Don't bet money with him. Or anything else you'd hate to lose."

"Very funny," Kate said. "I don't believe it. Who says so?"

"The caddies." Jake settled back down in his end of the boat.

"The caddies love him," Kate said. "Penny said they actively beg to go around with him."

"Sure, they do," Jake said. "He tips them so they won't rat on him. The per-capita income of caddies has gone up considerably since ol' Pete came to stay."

"I still don't believe it," Kate said, and slipped back down on her spine in her end of the boat. "He's just not the type."

Jake laughed, and she closed her eyes and ignored him. She could feel him watching her, but the water lapping at the side of the boat was so soothing that she forgot him and drifted off.

Jake tipped back his hat and watched her sleep. She looked a lot more vulnerable in her sleep. Almost like a kid. But she still looked cool and untouchable with her

hair all pulled back, dressed in those blah colors. There
was no heat in her. Which, when he considered it, was a
damn good thing because, her efficiency notwithstanding
and much against his better judgment, he could easily
have been attracted to her if he hadn't been married to
someone like her. He remembered Tiffany bitching at
him for taking life too easy. It had taken him a long while
to realize what the problem was, but he'd figured it out
eventually—she'd assumed she'd married somebody like
herself: career-driven, focused, successful. After a few
months of married life she'd realized that life was pretty
much a game to Jake, and she'd set out to change all
that. Well, she had. They were divorced before the year
was out.

The really sad thing was that neither one of them had
lied to the other or pretended to be anything but what
they were. They'd both just willfully misread each other
because of the raging physical attraction they'd felt. Jake
looked again at Kate curled peacefully at the other end
of the boat and reminded himself, *The physical stuff
doesn't last. Remember that, no matter what she does.*

Of course, he admitted to himself, Kate wasn't doing
anything. He'd mentally kicked himself for inviting her
into the boat, but she was turning out to be good company. Quiet except for the battle with the fish. A woman
who could take teasing without getting huffy, and who
didn't come on to him, didn't expect him to entertain her,
who just lay back in the boat and went to sleep. A truly
restful woman.

And she wasn't boring. In fact, she made a damn good
story. Last night at the luau, he'd found himself telling
his parents and uncle about Frank and Lance, with Will
putting in disclaimers. "You make her sound like the
Terminator," Will had said, laughing. "She is," he'd

said. But she didn't look dangerous now. She looked sort of…sexless. Like a kid sister. He'd never had a sister. Maybe he'd borrow Kate as a sister for the time she'd be around. It would be nice to have a friendship with a woman, and Kate would be absolutely safe because she was interested only in Yuppies, and he wasn't going to fall for her.

He looked over at Kate once more, shook his head, and then pulled his hat down and went to back to sleep.

When Kate woke up, it was late morning. She had rolled over on her side in her sleep, and their legs were tangled. She stretched and felt her legs slide along his. She thought idly about running her toe under the edge of his shorts and then blushed, deciding it was a very bad idea. She was sure she wasn't interested in him, and if he made a pass, they'd drown.

She pulled her legs back and sat up, suddenly feeling ravenous. Valerie had attacked her before she could eat breakfast, and it was still at least an hour short of lunch. She searched through the cooler. All it held was beer. Well, beer was nutritious, wasn't it? Hops and grain. She took one from the cooler and then leaned back to think about how pleasant life was on the lake, even with Jake there.

Well, actually, she admitted as she sipped the beer, Jake was probably one of the reasons it was pleasant. It was nice to have undemanding companionship, for a change. She watched him doze at the other end of the boat. He was like having a brother around. Like the brother she'd never had. Comfortable, fun to talk to, trustworthy. Well, more than that, maybe. She could get those qualities from an attentive dachshund. Of course, she'd never had a dachshund. What a shame.

She contemplated the idea of getting a dog over her second beer. It was probably a bad idea, since she lived in the city. Even if it was a little dog. It would be lonely in her apartment all day. She certainly was lonely in her apartment all night. *Stop it, Kate,* she told herself. *Self-pity is a sign of weakness.*

Kate leaned to put her empty can back in the pack and was getting her third when she realized that Jake wasn't sleeping anymore. She reached over and tilted his hat up, and he gazed sleepily back at her.

"Hello," she said. "Want a beer?"

"That would be nice."

She dropped the hat back over his eyes and cracked him a beer. He held out his hand, and she wrapped his fingers around it. He guided it back under his hat, and she cracked another can for herself and leaned back on the cushions. The sky was a brighter blue than before, and the sun had moved so that her end of the boat was partially in the sun. The heat warmed her white blouse uncomfortably. She drank her beer and envied Jake, cool without his shirt. One more unfair thing about civilization.

The third beer went down faster than the second because of the heat. Kate's head began to swim a little, probably because the sun was hot. She sat up and opened a fourth.

When he heard the crack of the pop-top, Jake lifted his hat for a moment and glanced at her, shrugged and lay back again.

Kate rolled the cold can against her throat and down the front of her blouse and thought about how unfair life was. It was really hot in the sun, but could she go topless? Noooo. And why? Because she was female. Life was sexist. And really, really unfair. She looked over at Jake, cool and comfortable and shirtless, and decided to strike a blow for women everywhere. *This is for all the hot women,* she thought, and took off her blouse. She was wearing a peach satin and white lace bra, the most conservative underwear Jessie had allowed her to buy. It covered, she reasoned, a lot more of her than a bikini top. She felt much better. She tossed her blouse into the center of the boat and leaned back to finish her beer.

Jake tilted his hat up when he felt her blouse hit his legs.

"Cooler?"

"Much."

"Try not to take anything else off. You'll scare the fish."

She waved her beer can at him and nodded, dabbling her hand in the water. "Here, fish."

"Kate, did you have any breakfast this morning?"

"Nope." She took another healthy swig of the beer.

He leaned forward and picked up the cooler, moving it out of her reach.

"Give me your beer," he said, and she moved to hand it to him, feeling her breasts tighten against the lace as she leaned forward. They felt wonderful.

Jake looked down as he took the can from her.

"Nice bra."

"Thank you. It's new."

He laughed. "Go back to sleep, kid. We'll go in when you wake up."

So much for sexless. Jake shook his head as he watched her. There was a lot of woman under that blouse. And there must have been something about Kate he'd missed, because he hadn't pegged her as a satin-and-lace type. Plain white cotton would have been his guess, although he hadn't guessed; Kate's underwear had never occurred to him because he'd never thought of Kate undressed.

She's repressed, he thought. *She wears all that tailored tan clothing and then wears sexy underwear underneath it.* But maybe *repressed* wasn't the right word. Maybe she was schizophrenic. It would explain why guys like Lance were splatting up against her like bugs on a windshield. The signals were there, and then she shot them down. Jake shook his head again, bewildered by her and at the same time smug that he, at least, was impervious to her charms. Still, he carefully avoided looking at her as she lay curled up, asleep, at the other end of the boat.

No point in pushing his luck.

An hour later, Kate woke up when Jake shook her foot to bring her out of her doze. She sat up and stretched clumsily, and he tossed her blouse to her. She put it on, missing the armhole the first time.

"Time to go home," he said.

"We should have brought lunch," Kate said.

"How do you feel?"

Kate considered it. Light-headed. Relaxed. Slightly turned-on. "I'm drunk."

"I'd guessed that. Button your blouse." He untied the boat and began to row back to shore. Kate concentrated on her blouse, watching her fingers push the buttons through the holes. *I wonder who thought of buttonholes,* she thought. *And I wonder what she was doing when she thought of them.* Visions of trains plunging into tunnels flashed through her head. She was still occupied with making the connection when Jake beached the boat, hauling it up onto the stones while she still sat in it. She climbed out, clumsily pulling the poles and the cooler bag with her.

"Wait a minute," he said and pulled her around to face him. "Who taught you to dress yourself?"

She had missed a couple of buttons. Big deal. She stood close to him while he straightened her shirt, popping the buttons out through the wrong holes and sliding them back through the right ones. Once his fingers touched her skin, and she instinctively leaned into him just a little, pressing slightly against his hands. He stopped for a minute and said, "Steady, kid," and then finished buttoning her blouse before he turned her around and sent her up the path with a little shove.

"Don't go too fast," he said. "I'm right behind you." He picked up the gear and took her up a different, much shorter path—one that brought them out above the cabins instead of past the hotel. Then he dropped the gear on her porch and asked her for her key.

"It's in my bra," she said and fished for it. It had slipped under her breast, but she found it and gave it to him, warm from her flesh.

"I'm surprised there was room for it in there," he said and unlocked her door.

She walked to her bed, wheeled around, waved to him to thank him, and fell backward onto the mattress. He picked up her feet and threw them up on the bed and then put his hands under her arms to haul her up onto the pillows.

He looked so cute bending over her with that mustache. She threw her arms around him and drew his face close to hers.

"You're the brother I never had," Kate said thickly.

"I can't tell you how good that makes me feel," Jake said, and then she passed out in his arms.

* * *

Jake went back to the hotel, shaking his head. The woman needed a keeper—any keeper but him. The memory of her—soft and round, with her arms around him—was disturbing. *Remember,* he told himself, *her body might be warm, but she has ice cubes in her eyes and a business plan for a heart.*

A vision of Kate smiling at him in the boat rose before him. Well, maybe she was more than that. She was friendly. And she was good company. And she didn't seem to have any ulterior motives. In fact, she thought of him as a brother. It made him feel both relieved and insulted because after all she was a damn attractive woman. And not nearly as icy as he'd thought. Her blue eyes had been melting when she'd smiled at him right before she'd passed out, cold as a haddock.

It didn't matter. He was going to stay away from her, that was the safest strategy, he resolved. She would be fine. She was playing golf this afternoon. How much trouble could she get into?

Then he remembered who she was playing golf with and sighed. She really did need a keeper.

An hour later, Kate woke up, still high from the beer, and went in search of food to counteract the alcohol. The big glassed-in dining room was crowded when she found it, so she was surprised to find Penny alone at a table for two.

"Oh, goody. Sit down, Kate. Please, sit down."

There was something gratifying about being that welcome, and Kate smiled as she joined her. Although not overly bright, Penny was truly a warm, open person and Kate wondered how she managed. With all the experience she must have had with men, how did she stay that trusting?

"No Chad?"

Penny shook her head. "He was Saturday. Today is Sunday."

"Like days-of-the-week underpants."

"Yeah." Penny giggled.

"Are you sure you want to get married?"

"Yes."

Kate waited for more explanation, but Penny just smiled at her—a smile as open and warm as the sun. The waiter brought Penny's salad.

"You want a salad, too, don't you Kate? Greg, could you be a honey and just hurry another salad over here for Kate?"

"You bet, Penny." The waiter beamed at her and shot back to the kitchen.

"It seems a shame to take you off the market," Kate said. "You bring such happiness to so many this way."

"I want a baby." Penny smiled at the thought.

"Oh. How about a husband? Want one of those, too?"

"Oh, sure." Penny seemed a lot less enthusiastic about the husband than the baby.

"Penny, I don't mean to pry, but do you love this man you're marrying?"

"Allan? Oh, sure."

"Does he, um, know you're here?"

"Oh, sure. He knows I like to dance and stuff, but he's very busy with his business. He knows I don't cheat or anything. Just dance and talk...you know. He likes me to have a good time."

"Oh."

Greg was back with Kate's salad. He never took his eyes off Penny while he served it to her, and Kate had to guide his hand at the last moment to keep the plate from sliding into her lap.

"Thanks."

"Yes, ma'am. Anything else?"

"Lunch," Kate suggested.

"Right. Right." Greg peeled his eyes from Penny. "What would you like?"

"A menu."

"Right. Right." Greg stole one from another table and gave it to her, his eyes zapping back to Penny like iron filings to a magnet.

"Turkey club sandwich," Kate said.

Greg smiled at Penny.

"Turkey club sandwich," Kate repeated.

Greg smiled at Penny.

"I think I'll have the turkey club sandwich," Kate said loudly.

"Right. Right." Greg backed toward the kitchen.

"Allan trusts me. He does get jealous sometimes, though," Penny admitted.

"I can't think why."

"The only thing I don't like about men is that they think they own you sometimes."

"That's the only thing you don't like?"

"What else is there?"

"I'll make you a list."

"No, really, men are fun." Penny played with her salad. "Men take care of you. It's nice."

"Does Allan take care of you?"

"Oh, yes." Penny sighed.

Kate watched her for a moment. "Penny, what's wrong with Allan?"

Penny hesitated and then put down her fork and leaned forward. "He's boring. Sometimes he'll be talking to me, and I'll just drift off and start thinking about clothes or babies or a movie I've seen. And then I'll remember he's talking, and I try to listen again.'' Penny came as close as she could to looking depressed. For Penny, this meant slightly less radiant. ''It doesn't really matter because he never notices, but...''

Kate winced, thinking of all the long silences in her own engagements. ''I was engaged to men like that. Three of them. So caught up in their own careers and their own ideas that they never even saw me. Don't marry him.''

''I have to marry somebody if I want kids. And I've known Allan since he moved next door when I was in the sixth grade and he was a senior.'' Penny sighed at the memory. ''He's smart. He's successful. He has a lot of money, and he'll take care of me and our children. No man is perfect, but Allan comes pretty close.'' She picked up her fork again. ''I'm not stupid. I know I'm not in love with him and that we won't have one of those happily-ever-after marriages. But I'm not like you. I don't want a career. I want to get married and have a lot of kids and stay home with them all the time.'' She took a bite of salad and chewed while she thought about what she wanted to say next. ''See, what I really want is to be a full-time mom. But if I marry somebody with not much money, I can't. I'll have to work. I mean, most husbands can't afford to have their wives not work. And Allan can. In fact, he wants me to stay home.''

''Oh,'' Kate said. ''Well...''

''I know. You think that's awful,'' Penny said.

''No,'' Kate lied. ''Not if it's what you really want.''

''I do.'' Penny bit her lip. ''I have this all planned out, and it will work. And I'll be fair to Allan. I do sort of love him and I'll take care of him, too, and I'll be a good wife. I just deserve these next two weeks. That's all.'' She looked at Kate. ''I suppose you think that's stupid.''

"I don't think you're stupid," Kate said, surprised to find she didn't. "I'm just not as honest as you are. But if you can be, I can be. I want that kind of marriage, too. The planned-out, practical kind. The only difference between the two of us is that I haven't found my Allan yet."

"So that's why you're here," Penny said. She looked around and leaned forward. "Well, this place is crawling with secure guys. You shouldn't have any problem finding one."

"So far, *crawling* is the right word for the men I've met," Kate said. "But I'm not giving up. I'm going to find a dependable, successful man if it kills me."

"I wish that didn't sound so boring," Penny said. "Why is security always boring?"

"Because if it were exciting, it wouldn't be safe," Kate said.

"So you're looking for a rich guy?"

"Well," Kate said, frowning. "Not rich. I don't care about money. I have money. But he has to be successful."

"Rich," Penny said, and ate some more salad.

"I guess so," Kate said. "You know, I really hate this. It seems so scheming. It *is* so scheming."

"I know," Penny said. "But you're not getting any younger. You're really good-looking for your age, but still, you'd better get somebody while you can."

"Thank you," Kate said.

Greg brought her lunch. Chicken salad.

"Can I get you anything else?" he asked, looking at Penny.

"No, thank you." Kate waited until he was gone and turned back to Penny. "From now on, don't come to the table until I've ordered, all right?"

Penny giggled.

"Is everything all right here?"

Kate looked up to find Valerie lurking near their table, looking cool, trim and professional in green linen.

"Fine," Kate said. "Everything's lovely."

"Good," Valerie said. "That's exactly how Will and I want you to feel."

"Will?"

"Will Templeton. My boss." Valerie smiled smugly. "And my fiancé."

"Congratulations," Kate said.

"Oh, sit down and tell us all about it," Penny said. "Will is really dishy. I didn't know you were engaged to him."

"Nobody knows," Valerie said, sliding into an empty chair. "Sometimes I don't think Will knows." She laughed shortly.

"Men," Penny said sympathetically. "They just don't know how to have a relationship."

"Oh, it's not that bad," Valerie said. "We're actually quite well matched. In three years, we haven't had one argument."

"Gee," Penny said. "Three years."

Valerie smiled at her smugly. "Will understands that I generally know what's best."

"I can't imagine being engaged for three years," Penny went on. "Why are you waiting so long to get married?"

Valerie glared at her.

"I was engaged for three years," Kate said. "Of course, I was engaged to three different men during that time. But that's a long time."

"A really long time," Penny said.

"Will and I have worked very hard to make this place

a success,'' Valerie snapped. "We haven't had time to consider anything else.''

"Working together," Kate said, conjuring up her own plan and seeing it made flesh in Will and Valerie. "That's wonderful. That's the kind of marriage I want—partners, working together to make a business grow." She looked over at Valerie. "That must be wonderful."

Valerie relaxed under Kate's blatant envy. "Well, it is, of course, but there are drawbacks. I mean, I am stuck here, after all, with nobody to talk to except the help, and they're hardly...well, you know."

Kate and Penny looked at each other and then at Valerie. "What?" Kate asked.

"Well, they're country people." Valerie wrinkled her nose. "They don't understand career women. Like us."

"Like us," Kate echoed, feeling vaguely insulted.

"Us?" Penny echoed too.

Valerie ignored her and stayed focused on Kate.

"I wanted to talk to you because I knew you'd understand."

"Understand?" *How much did I have to drink this morning?* Kate wondered. *How long is it going to take me to sober up? Why can't I comprehend what this woman is driving at?*

"I recognized you yesterday at the luau. I thought you looked familiar when you checked in. Then it hit me. Your picture was in *Business Week* last month. I pulled out my back copy and there you were." Valerie raised her eyebrows. "I'm very impressed."

"Don't be," Kate said. "I was in *Business Week* because I was standing next to my father when they took the picture."

"The caption said you were his successor. It must be wonderful, working with a powerful man like that."

"Oh, yes," Kate said. "Particularly when magazines start mentioning you as his successor. He loves that."

"I envy you. Living in the city. On the cutting edge. Sometimes I feel like I'm going to lose my mind, being stuck down here," Valerie said.

"Why do you stay?" Kate said.

Valerie shrugged. "This is where Will wants to be. And we're making this resort really take off. It's something we're doing together."

"Together," Kate said.

"Oh, yes," Valerie said. "And we've got so many ideas. Don't tell anyone," she added, dropping her voice, "but our next project is a real country bar. With jukeboxes and everything."

"Well, that sounds like fun," Kate said, trying to figure out why a country bar should be top secret.

"Isn't there a country bar in town?" Penny said.

"That's Nancy's," Valerie said. "She doesn't count. She doesn't have any idea how to run a business. She just opens the door and people come in and buy beer."

"Isn't that pretty much the idea behind running a bar?" Kate asked.

"Listen, that place could be a gold mine if she'd get her act together. Since she isn't," Valerie said, sitting back and smiling, "Will and I are going to open our own gold mine."

"What'll happen to Nancy?" Penny asked.

Valerie shrugged. "That's business."

"My father would like you," Kate said, drawing away from Valerie.

"Thank you," Valerie said.

"So when are you and Will getting married?" Penny asked.

"Soon," Valerie said. "I'm being recruited by a big

East Coast chain. When they make me an offer, I'll just tell Will. He's a very fair man. He couldn't possibly expect me to stay here indefinitely without some kind of commitment. And he can hardly run this place without me.''

Kate and Penny looked at each other again.

''Are you actually a partner here?'' Kate asked, confused. ''I'm not following you.''

Valerie frowned, annoyed at being pinned down. ''Will started this place over ten years ago. Five years ago, he expanded it with a silent partner who does absolutely nothing to help him run it. I came here three years ago when Will was about at his wits' end and saved him and the hotel by planning something besides golf for the guests. Remember the luau last night?''

Kate winced, remembering the luau, and nodded.

''Well, that was my idea. I have a lot of ideas like that. They bring a lot of people to this resort. I'm indispensable.''

''Lucky you,'' Kate said uneasily. She felt a sudden need to get far away from Valerie, as if she had something contagious that she might catch. Like maybe ruthless ambition and a total lack of humanity. She smiled brightly at Valerie and pushed back her chair. ''Well, I've got to run. I'm late to play golf.''

''Who are you playing with?'' Penny asked.

''Peter somebody.''

''Oh, he looks rich,'' Penny said. ''Good luck.''

''Good luck?'' Valerie raised her eyebrows at Kate.

''On my golf game,'' Kate said. ''I'm going to need all the luck I can get.''

''Well, then, I'll wish you good luck, too,'' Valerie said. ''Let's get together again later and talk. We've got so much in common.''

"That would be wonderful," Kate said, trying not to look appalled. "Really."

"Really," Valerie said. "I consider you as a role model."

"Wonderful," Kate said as she backed away. "I can't tell you how that makes me feel."

Four

I do not have anything in common with that woman, Kate told herself as she crossed the lobby. *And I am not her role model or anything else.* Then she caught sight of Peter waiting for her and stopped, startled by how familiar he looked as he came toward her. Who did he look like? Derek? Terence? Paul? All of them, she decided. Tall, distinguished, graying at the temples, determined, aggressive. He reached her with the same long strides her father always took and put his arm around her and looked down at her, smiling. She hated it when men did that. She always felt small.

"You look fantastic. I'll have to show you off to everyone," Peter said, and she stared up at him for a moment, speechless with dismay. Now that he was close, he didn't really look all that much like any of the men she'd been engaged to. It was more the way he moved, looming over her, beaming at her. As if she was something he'd achieved.

"Um, wait a minute," she said, and automatically backed off toward the lobby desk to get away from him. When she backed into the desk with a bump, she realized she'd left him standing in the middle of the lobby, confused and annoyed. *Snap out of it,* she told herself. *You're acting like a fool. There is nothing wrong with this man. What's wrong with you?*

He cheats, Jake had said. And for some reason, she suddenly trusted Jake in his dumb cowboy hat and ratty shorts more than she trusted this man in tailored flannels.

On an impulse, she called Will over to the desk.

"Do you have any field glasses?"

"Just small ones." Will reached under the counter for a pair of miniature folding binoculars. "They're no good for bird-watching. I can hunt up some bigger ones for you if you're not in a hurry." He gave her an open, friendly smile that confused Kate. What was a nice man like this doing destroying neighborhood bars with a barracuda like Valerie?

"Kate?" Will said as she stared at him.

"These will be fine," she said. "The bird I'm watching is pretty big." She slipped them in her pocket and went back to Peter, who was pointedly looking at his watch.

They walked toward the course, Peter nodding right and left to acquaintances, always keeping a proprietary hand on her back as if she were his entry in a particularly prestigious pet show. *He's in public relations,* Kate remembered. *Maybe he considers me good for his image.*

"The flat Toby's Corners course is a good amateur course," Peter informed her when they reached the hill course. He signaled to a couple of caddies. "However, if you've had any experience at all, we should golf on this course." He smiled down at her, patronizing her and challenging her at the same time. "This one is more demanding."

Kate smiled back warily.

"Of course, it's not as impossible as everyone claims it is." Peter chuckled and handed his bag and the bag he'd rented for her to the caddies without looking at them. "In fact," he added, "I've been scoring under par pretty regularly here."

The caddies were about twenty, and the redheaded one looked familiar. Kate saw them look at each other and grin when Peter announced that he played under par. Score one for Jake. How did she find these men?

These men are what you're looking for, aren't they? Tall, distinguished, successful, and rich. You just forgot to put "honest" in your job description.

"How about a little bet?" Peter was looking at her guilelessly. "I'll even add ten points to my handicap."

Her father always smiled like that just before he closed a deal. She had always hated that smile. How could she get out of this date?

"You have played before?" Peter asked.

"Oh, once or twice," she said, adding silently, *since college when I was on the golf team.* The problem was that college was fourteen years ago.

"How about fifty bucks?" he asked.

I can't believe this, Kate thought. *He's trying to set me up. And then he'll probably try to make me. Well, the hell with you, Peter-Derek-Paul-Terence. I'm tired of being used by men like you. This time, I'm going to win. And I'm not just talking about golf.*

She beamed up at him. "How about a hundred?" she countered.

Peter beamed back. "Fine, fine."

Her redheaded caddie was gently shaking his head at her, and she winked. His eyes widened and he exchanged glances with the other caddie.

Peter's first drive hooked into a nearby field. As he and his caddie trailed to where the ball had gone in, Kate took out her field glasses, keeping them hidden in her hand. When they reached the field, Peter waved to her and went to find his ball. Kate brought the glasses up and saw him kick the ball back out of the rough.

"I do believe that my opponent's ball just took another bounce," she murmured to her caddie.

"Your opponent's balls tend to do that," her caddie said.

"Do they, now? I'm Kate." She offered him her hand.

"I'm Mark," he said, taking it.

"The bartender," Kate said, remembering. "Is there anything you don't do here?"

"Not much," Mark said cheerfully. "I'm studying hotel management, and Will wants me learning from the ground up."

Kate surveyed the hill straight ahead. "Well, the ground here certainly goes up."

"The better to cheat you on." Kate looked back at him sharply, and Mark nodded. "Unfortunately true. I think you're going to lose a hundred dollars."

"Oh, no," Kate said. "I'm used to fighting uphill battles. And I was brought up to be a winner. Daddy wouldn't settle for anything less."

She teed up her ball and hit it sweetly onto the green.

"I've got a feeling I'm going to enjoy this round," Mark said.

"Oh, me, too," Kate said.

She realized early in the game that she could have beaten Peter easily if he'd played fair, but his cheating evened things up considerably. Kate wasn't surprised. That was probably how he'd gotten where he was today. After all, most rich men didn't get that way by refusing to cut corners; they took every advantage they got. That's what she'd liked about them. They were aggressive. Hard-hitting.

God, I'm dumb, she thought.

Peter smiled at her condescendingly.

But she wasn't as dumb as he was. She smiled back. Two could play that game. With that thought in mind, on the fourth hole when she sliced into the rough, she kicked her ball back out without any compunction at all.

Peter looked astonished when he saw her ball. "Weren't you in the rough?"

"Lucky bounce," Kate said.

Mark nodded solemnly.

Peter scowled at her and went back to his ball.

"This is getting nasty," Mark said. "Personally, I like it. Too bad Jake isn't here to see this."

Kate frowned at him. "Jake?"

Mark opened his mouth and closed it again.

"Tell me," Kate said, and Mark shrugged.

"Jake sent me out here to look after you," he said. "He figured you wouldn't listen to him, so…"

"So you're baby-sitting." Kate sighed.

"Don't mention I told you," Mark said.

"Told me what?" Kate widened her eyes at him. "Now, get out of my way, sonny. I'm a woman on a mission."

The game degenerated into the kind of game the CIA would play—covert golf. They both preferred to hit when the other's back was turned. As the game progressed and the cheating grew more blatant, Kate shook her hair out of her chignon and laughed, and Peter began to look frantic.

"This is the only way to play golf," Kate said to Mark. "And it took me until now to discover it. I'm going to take this jerk to dinner tonight in gratitude."

"I don't think he's going to make it to dinner." Mark

watched Peter, frowning. "He's never lost before. And he's never turned that color before, either."

"He's fine," Kate said. "There's only one more hole."

Peter choked on his swing again, and his ball disappeared into the brush. He stalked off after it, leaving his caddie in the lurch with Kate and Mark.

The problem with men like Peter was that they always got away with their slimy little tricks. That wasn't fair. Something had to be done about that.

"Let's go watch this time," Kate said, and the three of them trailed silently after him.

They got to the edge of the course just in time to see Peter kick his ball savagely back onto the green.

"Why, Pete," Kate said brightly. "That's cheating."

He jerked back at the sound of her voice and stared at her in anguish, and his face went gray. "Kate," he croaked, and then he collapsed.

"Peter?" Kate bent over him. "Peter, it's a dumb game. Nobody cares. Peter?"

She went down on her knees beside him. He wasn't breathing.

"Call 911," Kate ordered Mark and bent to give Peter mouth-to-mouth.

Half an hour later, Jake stood beside her on the green and shook his head as the ambulance pulled away. "First Lance, now this," he said.

"We gave him CPR. He's going to be all right," Kate said. "The doctor said so."

"Dating you is like dating death," Jake said.

Kate looked exasperated. "Nobody has died."

"Not yet."

Kate started to say something cutting and then remembered that Jake had sent Mark to look out for her. She was used to men who said nice things to her and left her to fend for herself. A man who implied she was a menace and then took care of her was a new experience.

"I forgive you," Kate said. "You're a good person." She patted him on the arm and then strolled off in the direction of her cabin.

"What?" Jake said, confused, but she was gone.

"You should have been there," Mark told him and Will later. "That woman needs protecting like Rambo needs a bodyguard."

"I didn't think she'd listened to me," Jake said. "My mistake."

"I don't think she misses much," Mark said.

"Well, don't tell her I sent you," Jake said. "I don't want her getting any ideas."

"Right," Mark said, turning swiftly away. "I sure won't. Well, gotta go."

"What's wrong with him?" Jake asked as Mark ducked out the office door.

"What's wrong with you?" Will countered. "What do you mean, you don't want her getting any ideas? You should be so lucky." He shook his head. "I worry about you sometimes, bro. Kate Svenson's a damn good-looking woman and you don't seem to have noticed. You're getting close to legally dead, here."

"I'll be a lot closer if I get interested in her, and so will you. She's the one who put Lance in the pool last night, remember?"

"Good for her," Will said.

"Well, I don't intend to be her next victim."

"I don't know," Will said, considering. "She's something else. It wouldn't be a bad way to go."

"Hey," Jake said, annoyed. "You stick to Valerie. If anything happens to you, I own all of this monstrosity instead of just half."

"With any luck at all, Valerie will unstick herself," Will said. "That idiot Donald Prescott who's been telling everybody that he's a stockbroker is really the scout for Eastern Hotels. He's trying to get her under contract."

Jake raised his eyebrows. "And how did you find this out?"

Will shook his head in disgust. "I met him at that convention in New Orleans last year. He, of course, doesn't remember since he has the mental capacity of a gnat."

Jake grinned. "And it doesn't bother you that the gnat is trying to steal your woman?"

Will sank down into his desk chair and put his head in his hands. "I should be so lucky. Do you know what her latest harebrained idea is? To put in a new bar and drive Nancy out of business."

Jake snorted. "And just how does she plan to do that?"

"Oh, she wants to build a real country bar," Will said, shaking his head. "Can you imagine anything so dumb? Nancy's has been a real country bar for more than thirty years. So Valerie wants us to build a fake country bar to drive her out of business. Even assuming I'd go along with it, which she must have known I wouldn't, this is a dumb idea."

"So what did she say when you said no?"

"She got that look," Will said. "The old 'We'll see' look she gets every time I don't agree with her."

"I hate that look," Jake said.

"You know, I really appreciate what Valerie's done for this place—"

"I don't."

"But she's really been getting to me lately." Will hesitated. "I started to pay more attention after I talked to you yesterday, and I think you're right. I think she wants to get married." He looked at Jake in bafflement. "Can you believe it?"

Jake closed his eyes in disgust. "Of course, I can believe it. You've lived with her for three years. What did you think she wanted?"

"To build the biggest resort in the Midwest," Will said. "That's all she ever talks about. If she'd been making noises about kids or something, I'd have caught on sooner. But all she ever talked about was the resort, which was fine by me." He looked up at Jake. "She's talking about expanding my suite—which, by the way, she calls *our* suite—into the one next door. So we'd have two bedrooms. I said, why? It's not like we don't have any place to put guests, and she said, 'I'm not talking about guests.'" He put his head in his hands. "I think she means kids," he said hollowly. "How did I get into this mess?"

"Not that I'm in favor of you marrying Valerie," Jake said, "but you have been sleeping with her for quite some time now."

Will looked at him blankly. "So?"

"So I don't think all she thinks about is the resort," Jake said. "I thought you were supposed to be the quick one in the family."

"I am," Will said. "What's your point?"

Jake closed his eyes. "Never mind. Just pray that Donald what's-his-name gets her out of here before she realizes that you're never going to marry her, and she decides to kill you."

"Valerie wouldn't do anything that emotional," Will said. "You're getting her confused with Kate."

"I will never confuse Kate with Valerie," Jake said. "They're completely different."

Kate went back to the cabin and tried to feel ashamed of what she'd done. It didn't work.

Maybe she wasn't meant to be married. A woman who truly wanted to get married would have let Peter win. She shook her head. She'd never want to get married *that* much.

On the other hand, the afternoon was hardly a sign that she should give up. Lance and Peter were jerks. That didn't mean the rest of the men here were. In fact, the law of averages said that she had to do better next time.

Maybe she should focus her plan better. What she wanted was somebody distinguished and successful who was also caring and honest. Sort of a cross between her father and Jake. She tried to imagine what that cross would look like and couldn't. It was like trying to cross a shark with a teddy bear. She gave up and was heading for the shower when the phone rang.

"Kate?" Jessie said. "Are you engaged yet?"

"Of course not," Kate said. "Why are you calling?"

"You've been there twenty-four hours," Jessie said. "I wanted to know if it was time to start baking the wedding cake."

"Very funny," Kate said.

"I have the perfect design," Jessie said. "A tasteful stack of staggered sheet cakes decorated to look like government bonds, artfully garnished with roses made from folded hundred-dollar bills."

"Listen, if all I was after was money, I'd have stuck to the first two men I met here," Kate said.

"Oh, good. Tell me everything."

"No. It was depressing. What have you been doing?"

"Coating two ring cakes with edible gold powder for the Dershowitzes' fiftieth anniversary. You should see the cherubs I've made to go on top. They look just like the Dershowitzes. Even I'm impressed with how incredible I am."

Kate bit her lip. "Jessie, do you ever have doubts about what you want? You know, about your goals?"

"What goals?" Jessie said. "Goals are for fascists. Are you having doubts about your goals? Because, if so, it's about time."

"Well, not really…"

"Let me guess. You've met some distinguished, rich guys, and they're not much fun, and you've seen the error of your ways."

"No." Kate hesitated. "Well, I've had two dates that were…well…mistakes, I guess."

"But you behaved beautifully," Jessie said with obvious disgust. "Even though they were boring and shallow, you smiled and were the perfect lady."

"No. I pushed one in the pool and gave the other one a heart attack on the golf course."

"What?"

"He reminded me a lot of the men I was engaged to."

"A heart attack?"

"Do you think that's why I tried to kill Peter today on the golf course?"

"Wait a minute. Are we talking actual death, here?"

"No. Jake showed up and helped me give him mouth-to-mouth and then the paramedics came."

"Who's Jake?"

"Nobody. Anyway, Peter's fine now."

"So, let me get this straight. You tried to kill this guy

because he reminded you of the three stooges you were engaged to? This vacation was really a *very* good idea.''

''Well, I didn't actually try to kill him. I just beat him at golf.''

''If he's like the stooges, that would do it.''

''He is. It did. He deserved it. He cheated.''

''And you caught him. Good girl.''

''Well, Jake told me he would. And then—''

''Who's Jake?''

''Nobody. And then when I cheated, too—''

''You cheated? You?''

''It seemed fair. He was.''

''Excuse me. You *are* Kate Svenson, right?''

''You know, perhaps it was all the beer I had this morning.''

''You drank beer in the morning?''

''It was all Jake packed, and I was stuck in the middle of the lake in this decaying rowboat—''

''Who's Jake?''

''Forget Jake. He's not interesting.''

''The hell he isn't. *I'm* interested.''

''He's some kind of handyman.'' Kate stopped to think. ''You know, I'm not sure what he does.''

There was a long silence on the other end of the phone.

''Jessie?''

''You spent the morning drinking beer on a lake in a rowboat with a man, and you're not sure what he does but you think he's a handyman.''

''Right.''

''Maybe I'd better drive down,'' Jessie said. ''This is not like you.''

''I'm fine,'' Kate said. ''In fact, since my last two dates were so awful, things can only get better.''

"Bad deduction," Jessie said. "If that were true, I'd be dating Harrison Ford by now."

"I'm still not giving up," Kate said. "I'm just modifying my plan slightly."

"Modify all you want," Jessie said. "The more changes you make in that plan, the better. Just don't do anything drastic without checking in with me."

"Because you know so much about men? You forget I know all about your pathetic love life," Kate said.

"At least I occasionally have one," Jessie said. "You're still planning the perfect business merger. A little more love would do you a world of good. Why don't you forget that plan and just fall in love?"

"Right," Kate sneered. "And then I'd end up with some loser like…"

"Like?"

"Forget it."

"Tell me more about Jake," Jessie said.

"Forget Jake. He's not a possibility. There are some others who are. This could still work out." There was Donald what's-his-name. And Eric. And Rick was very nice. "Jessie?" Kate added, after a pause.

"Yeah?"

"Thanks for sending me down here. I think I'm having a good time."

"Yeah, well, call me when you're sure," Jessie said. "You're behaving very strangely."

"I think that's why I'm having a good time," Kate said.

Kate found Penny at the pool later that afternoon, barely dressed in a lime-green bikini and surrounded by men. She stretched out next to her on a lounge chair and surveyed the scene with contentment. Mark had the bar set up again, and people drifted by, socializing in the lazy Sunday afternoon, smelling of suntan lotion, chlorine, and booze. They were the same people who had annoyed Kate so the day before, but she smiled at them now as they went past, and they smiled back.

Jake and Will sat at the end of the bar, arguing over some papers. Jake was in torn jeans and a white T-shirt with the label sticking up in back. He did nice things for a plain old T-shirt, not to mention the jeans, and she felt a moment's regret that he didn't fit her plan. Will looked cool and distinguished in tailored slacks and a well-cut shirt; no wonder Valerie was doing everything she could to hold on to him. Strange men to be friends, so different, although now that she studied them, they did sort of look alike.

Frank, rounder than usual in bright red shorts and a tank top, was attempting to pick up two college girls sunning on the other side of the pool. They politely ignored him, although Kate noticed that one, a trim little brunette, kept an eye on Jake and Will. She'd better settle for Jake. Valerie would not be amused if someone moved in on her future. The idea of Jake and the college girl was annoying for some reason, but before she could pursue it further, one of Penny's men, a tall blond she remembered vaguely from the night before, attached himself to her.

"Calvin Klein's resort collection." He surveyed her outfit with approval.

She studied him over her sunglasses. He wore horn-rimmed glasses, which made him endearingly attractive. His blond hair was beautifully cut. His tan slacks were impeccably tailored. He was keeping his hands to himself. And best of all, so far he hadn't challenged her to anything.

She held out her hand. "Kate Svenson."

"I'm Donald Prescott." He took her hand and smiled into her eyes. "We met yesterday at the luau. You look marvelous. It can't be easy to look that cool and collected at a country pool. You really have presence."

"Thank you, Donald." Presence. She'd rather have sex appeal. She glanced over at Penny in her string bikini. Penny had no presence at all. Penny had fun.

Penny waved at her. "I'm so glad you're here," she said and Kate was taken aback for a moment at the sincerity in her voice. Penny was a truly good, warm person. Her values were a little whacked out, but her heart was sound. She should be nicer to Penny. In fact, she should be more *like* Penny.

Donald caught her attention briefly by telling her about a Donna Karan outlet only a few hours from the hotel. Given the savings, he insisted, the drive was an economically sound choice. "She really does make the best suits for women," he said. "But of course you know that."

"Of course," Kate said, distracted by the little brunette who was moving with purpose toward the bar.

Donald claimed her attention again, and he told her about prices in the city and the best place to buy jewelry.

Donald's very nice, she thought, *and very good-looking, and I should concentrate on what I came here for. What is that brunette doing?*

Kate watched while Will poured the girl a soda, smiling at her before he went back to Jake and the paperwork. The girl dawdled on her way back to her chair. Neither Jake nor Will noticed. Good. They were too old for her, anyway.

Jake leaned on the bar and talked to Will, pointing something out in the papers in front of them. Their heads were close, their hair the same dark, dark brown.

"Jake looks a lot like Will," she said to Penny. "They could be brothers."

"They are," Penny said. "I wish I had a hat.'

Kate looked back at Jake, confused. "Jake works as a handyman in his brother's hotel?"

"Jake's an accountant. He just helps around here every now and then because Will owns the hotel. I think Will lets him live in the last cabin for free."

Kate frowned. "Jake's an accountant?"

"He used to be some kind of tax lawyer in Boston. Then he came home, and now he helps Will with the hotel and does everybody else's taxes. Isn't his cowboy hat the coolest?"

"Jake was a tax attorney?"

"I think he made a lot of money and retired or something." Penny pulled a mirror from her bag and checked her makeup. "Let's go to that bar tonight that Valerie was talking about. Nancy's."

"It's Sunday. It's not open." Kate stared at Jake. "Jake was a tax attorney?"

"What difference does it make? He's not anymore." Penny took out her lipstick and carefully darkened her beautiful lips. "Maybe we can go to the bar tomorrow night. I think somebody should warn Nancy that Valerie is trying to run her out of business."

"I don't know, Penny," Kate said, still watching Jake. "It might be better not to get in the middle of that."

"Well, let's just go and see," Penny said. "I want to meet Nancy anyway. Everybody says she's really nice. Will you come with me?"

"Sure," Kate said absently. Jake and Will were nodding at each other and then Will went down the length of the bar to serve another guest. Jake went back to the papers, making notes on a separate page while he studied

the figures in front of him. For a moment, Kate could see
him as he must have been before—focused, alert, intelligent, and professional. Then Jake seemed to catch himself. He looked down at his notes, shook his head, and
crumpled up the paper, closed the ledger. When Will re-
turned, he shoved the rest of the paperwork back to him
with one finger as if it were unclean.

He was too young to retire, but there he was, not doing
much of anything, a tax attorney who mowed lawns. And
he was lazy and unmotivated, but he showed up on the
golf course knowing CPR. And he was Will's unem-
ployed brother, but Will listened to him, as if he were a
partner. And he was definitely not her type, yet she was
more comfortable with him than with any other man
she'd ever met.

Strange man.

Donald claimed her attention again.

"There's a store in the village that sells hats like
Jake's," he told her and Penny.

"Super," Penny said, looking at him.

"Super," Kate echoed, looking at Jake.

Five

At nine the next morning—ignoring her own nagging doubts that she was wasting time she could better use furthering her plan—Kate met Jake at the lake.

"Valerie just called my cabin to arrange a nature hike," she said. "Please don't let her get me. I brought a book. I won't annoy you."

"You don't annoy me," Jake said. "Get in."

He rowed them across the lake and back under the willows, stripped off his shirt and lay back to sleep, just as he had the morning before.

"Is this all you do?" Kate asked, settling herself with her book.

"What?"

"Sleep in boats?"

Jake tipped his hat back and scowled at her from his end of the boat. "I get up at five-thirty and work my butt off making sure the grounds look nice for people like you, and this is the thanks I get?"

"Sorry," Kate said.

Jake nodded once and put his hat back over his face.

"So what is it you do, exactly?"

Jake tipped his hat back again. "If you're going to be chatty, I'm rowing you back to shore."

Kate shrugged. "I'm just curious. Penny said you used to be a tax attorney."

"*Used to be* are the operative words," Jake said. "Now I'm in outdoor management." He put his hat back.

"Does that mean you mow lawns?"

"No, that means I tell other people to mow lawns. Now shut up and let me sleep."

Kate opened her book, but ended up daydreaming instead. It was so peaceful on the lake, no pressures, no stress. Just the lake and the fish and Jake. She recalled the things she'd planned with Jessie back in the city and smiled. Jake would think she was insane if she told him.

She looked over at him. He wasn't breathing deeply enough to be asleep yet.

"Have you ever noticed how reality changes, depending on where you are?" she asked him.

"No."

"When I was in the city, I had an idea of the way things should be that seemed perfectly logical. But then I came to Toby's Corners and my idea didn't seem... well...quite right. And then I row out here with you, and in the middle of the lake, that same idea seems so stupid, it's funny. Do you know what I mean?"

Jake was quiet for so long that she assumed he'd fallen asleep. Abruptly, he said, "Yes."

"What?" Kate asked, startled.

"Yes, I know what you mean." Jake pushed his hat off his face again. "That's why I don't go into cities and why I spend a lot of time out here."

"Oh," Kate said. "What was your stupid city idea?"

"That money was good, and it would be fun to make some," Jake said.

"Oh," Kate said again. After a moment, she added, "That was a stupid idea?"

"Well, not in Boston," Jake said. "In Boston, they thought I was a wonder."

"But not here?"

"Well…" Jake stretched a little. "Toby's Corners has a very practical idea of money. It's the stuff you use to pay the rent and buy food. In the city, it was more a way of keeping score."

"Isn't that just because there's more of it in the city?" Kate said.

"No," Jake said. "For instance, take my Aunt Clara. Now she was rich by Toby's Corners standards, and when she died she split her money between Will and me."

"That was nice of her," Kate said.

"Well, it came to about twenty thousand dollars apiece, which was a fortune here but not much to brag about where I was living." Jake reached over and opened the cooler. "I am having a beer," he said. "You are having juice." He handed her a can of orange juice and leaned back.

"Thank you," Kate said, repressing her retort so she could hear the rest of the story. "So what happened next?"

"Well, I was divorced and was making more than I could ever spend, and I was living in the city instead of Toby's Corners, so it was like Monopoly money for me. For a couple of years, I played the market. I lost a little, won a lot, lost a little, won a lot. It was fun. Like playing a game."

Jake had fallen silent so Kate nudged him with her foot again.

"Go on," she prompted.

"Well," he said slowly, "meanwhile back here, Will was taking correspondence courses in hotel management, planning to open up this old eight-cabin motel that had been deserted for as long as anybody could remember.

Since he was in Toby's Corners instead of the city, he used his money to buy up some land and repair the cabins, which of course was a really dumb investment by city standards. The family dug up some old furniture to fill them up, and he advertised and some vacationers showed up. He built some more cabins, and then he borrowed from the bank and put in the little golf course behind them. Things went pretty well for him, but he wasn't making what the city would call real money. He was just giving some people around here some jobs and supporting himself. Barely.''

"So you were in the fast lane, and he was in the slow," Kate said.

"Well, Will and I always were different," Jake said. "Although actually, it's usually been the other way around. I've always been a loper, and he's always been a sprinter. But I couldn't wait to get out of here, and he couldn't stand to leave."

"So how did you end up back here mowing lawns?"

"I'm getting to that," Jake said. "You sure you're interested in this?"

"Fascinated," Kate said.

Jake drank another slug of beer. "Where was I? Oh yeah, Will was hiring some people from the town to work up here, and as the place got bigger, so did the size of the staff. Pretty soon, he was the local tycoon. So when everything went to hell, they came to him."

"Went to hell?"

"Well, most of our people worked at the plant over at Tuttle," Jake said. "Little town, about fifteen miles north of here?"

Kate remembered it vaguely from her drive down—a lost, gray place full of empty stores and houses. "What happened?"

"Plant closed. Owners moved the whole operation to Mexico."

"Ouch," Kate said. "How many jobs?"

"About three hundred, give or take a few," Jake said. He looked grim for a minute. "They just moved out; no warning at all."

"So what happened?" Kate said.

"Well, people started showing up, asking Will for work, but of course, there was no way he could hire that many people. But they were all looking at him, and you know Will." Jake looked over at her. "Well, actually, you don't know Will. He thinks he's everybody's daddy, Will does."

Kate thought about Will and Valerie taking over Nancy's bar. "But..."

"But what?"

"Never mind." Kate shook her head, confused. "What happened next?"

"Oh, he did what he always did when we were kids and he got into trouble—he called me."

"And you saved the day."

Jake snorted. "Hell, no. I was clueless and told him so. And he said he didn't want a clue, he wanted money. A lot of it. And he asked me to fix him up with some investment types so he could build a resort that would keep people in jobs."

"Oh," Kate said. "This changes the way I look at the resort."

"Yeah," Jake said. "Every time I look at that damn plywood Taj Mahal, I think about the jobs, and I shut up."

"So you found him the backers."

"No," Jake said, taking another drink from his can. "I just gave him all the money I had and came home."

''You must have had a lot of money.''

''Will was impressed,'' Jake said.

''This resort employs three hundred people?''

''Well, it did while it was being built,'' Jake said. ''And then with all the people coming in, the stores in town started to do a nice business in antiques and crafts and that kind of crap. And every time Valerie stages one of her stunts like that godawful luau, we hire everybody for miles around to help out. All in all, Will pretty well saved old Toby's Corners.''

''Will and you,'' Kate corrected him.

''Nope,'' Jake said, pulling his hat back over his eyes. ''Just Will. It was pure dumb luck that I was on a major roll in the market right then. Another time, I could have been flatter than roadkill.''

''And you don't ever think about going back,'' Kate said.

''Nope.''

''You must have been pretty good,'' Kate said. ''To have made all that money, I mean.''

Jake tilted his hat back and glared at her. ''Well, I don't have any now, so don't start getting ideas.''

''Like what?'' Kate asked, stung.

''Like I'm a Yuppie you might be interested in.''

Kate was speechless for a moment.

''I know your kind, lady,'' Jake said. ''You eat guys like me for breakfast. Well, forget it. I'm broke.'' He went back under his hat.

Kate considered kicking him, but decided it would be unladylike. ''You know, I find it absolutely amazing that this boat doesn't sink under the weight of your ego.''

''Ha.''

''The only reason I might possibly be interested in you is because you helped your brother save this town. Since you obviously didn't, there is absolutely nothing about a shaggy, lazy, arrogant, macho blowhard like you to attract me.''

"Shaggy?"

"Your hair and your mustache need trimming."

"Now, see," Jake said. "That is just the kind of attitude that made me leave the city."

"Also that cowboy hat is ridiculous."

"Hey." Jake tipped the hat back. "Will gave me this hat. It is not ridiculous."

"Why would he give you a dumb hat?"

"Because he said I was a hero," Jake mumbled.

"What?"

"He said if I was going to act like a guy in a white hat and rescue everybody, I should have a white hat," Jake said.

Kate laughed softly, and he glared at her.

"So that's why you wear it all the time," Kate said. "You big fake."

"What?"

"You love being back here and knowing you're half of the save-the-day Templeton brothers. You wear that hat because you're proud of being a big hero. And then you go around saying, 'Aw, shucks, ma'am, it twern't nothin,' and insulting perfectly innocent people from the city like me."

"You are not perfectly innocent," Jake said.

"I certainly am," Kate said. "I can't believe you think I'd make a play for you just because you have money."

"I don't have any money," Jake said.

"Well, I do," Kate said. "Lots of it."

"How much?" Jake said. "I may make you start paying for the beer."

"Not unless I get to drink some of it," Kate said. "Did you really think I'd jump you for your money?"

"I have it on good authority that you're up here looking for a rich businessman," Jake said. "That ain't me."

"What good authority?" Kate said, startled.

"Valerie told Will."

"Oh, hell," Kate said.

Jake shook his head. "Women."

"Well, that was the idea I was talking about," Kate said. "The one that seemed great in the city and stupid here."

"Stay out of cities," Jake advised. "They have a worse effect on your brain than they do on mine."

"Well, it wasn't completely stupid," Kate said. "I'm thirty-five. I want to get married, and that stuff they kept telling me about the right man suddenly appearing before me just wasn't happening. So I decided to get serious about it."

"And you came down here to get engaged to a suit," Jake said.

"No, I've been engaged to suits. Three of them. I came down here to find someone I could seriously consider marrying." Kate looked at him with narrowed eyes. "You are not him. Relax and drink your beer."

"You were engaged three times?" Jake started to laugh. "What made them leave?"

"They didn't. I did." Kate tried to look detached and failed miserably. "I couldn't bring myself to go through with it."

"I still don't get why you came down here. Why didn't you just go down to a nice big investment-banking firm and hang around the men's room until somebody who looked good came out?"

"Fine, laugh at me," Kate said. "At least I'm doing

something about my empty life instead of mowing lawns and hiding out on lakes."

"I don't mow the lawns," Jake said. "I supervise other people mowing lawns. It's a management-level position. Also I own half of the resort, but the investment isn't liquid so you're not interested."

"I don't care if it's vapor. I'll never be interested." Kate glared at him. "I can't believe I'm listening to this."

"Also, don't look now, but you're hiding out on this lake, too, kiddo. We are both, so to speak, in the same boat."

"Yes, but this afternoon, I will be pursuing my plan while you go rot in the azaleas."

"We don't have azaleas," Jake said. "What are you doing this afternoon?"

"Shopping in town with Donald Prescott, who is a stockbroker and possibly the man of my dreams," Kate said.

"No, he's not," Jake said.

"Excuse me," Kate said, "but I will determine my own dreams. You, by the way, are not in them."

"He's not a stockbroker," Jake said. "You really can pick them."

"He says he's a stockbroker," Kate said.

Jake looked at her sadly. "Do not believe everything men tell you, dummy," he said. "He's a scout for Eastern Hotels. He's here to hire Valerie away from Will."

Kate blinked. "What's Will doing about it?"

"Praying that he hurries up," Jake said.

"Aren't they engaged?"

Jake snorted. "Who told you that fairy tale?"

"Valerie."

Jake closed his eyes. "Well, I warned him."

"What?"

"Forget Will and Valerie. Explain to me this plan of yours so I can avoid it."

"You're not even in the running," Kate said. "I'm looking for someone tall, successful and distinguished."

"I'm tall," Jake said.

"You slump," Kate said. "Forget it."

"So tell me again why you came here of all places?"

"My best friend sent me. She thought it was a great idea. She, of course, is not here and has never been here, so she didn't realize I'd end up on a lake with a bozo like you."

"And this friend is an expert on men?"

"Jessie? Good heavens, no. She dates even bigger losers than I do." Kate surveyed him critically. "She'd like you."

"On that note," Jake said, "I am going to sleep. Wake me up when it's time for your date with Donald."

"I certainly will," Kate said. "It's going to be wonderful, and I don't want to miss a moment."

At two, Kate met Donald and Penny and a new friend of Penny's named Brian, and they all drove into town together.

The town was wonderful.

Donald was awful.

He was tall, looming over her in his designer suit. He was distinguished, his cologne discreetly exclusive, his hair cut strand by strand by a trendy stylist. He was successful, everything about him shrieking designer labels and money. He was detached, reserved and worldly. And he was, above all, what Kate would once have called discerning.

By the end of the afternoon, she had acquired a different, unprintable adjective for him.

They went first into a store called The Toby's Corners Shop. It was crammed floor to ceiling with gifts and souvenirs in colors Mother Nature never made, and Kate drew back, her good taste offended by the cheapness of it all. Penny picked out a pink stuffed dog with a tag around his neck that said "Toby," and Brian bought it for her. She hugged him to thank him, and he closed his eyes in ecstasy and hugged back.

Donald was patient while they looked through the store, although he told them firmly in a voice that carried from one end of the place to the other that the store was just an overpriced tourist trap. The little old man who ran it looked wounded, so Kate bought Jessie a neon-purple T-shirt that said "Somebody Went To Toby's Corners And All I Got Was This Lousy T-shirt," and an ashtray for her father that looked like a dog leaning against a tree.

"I really love your shop," she told the old man to make up for Donald, and he smiled at her and thanked her and told her about how he and his wife had been running it for almost two years now, to help with their retirement.

Donald waited with ill-disguised patience by the door.

Then they went into The Corners Art Gallery and looked at walls hung with garish landscapes. Kate tried hard to think about all the work that had gone into the paintings instead of about how bad they were. Donald examined the paintings closely. "Amateur brushwork," he announced. "Paint By Numbers stuff." The young man behind the counter looked ready to defend his art with his fists, so Kate asked if he had any pictures of the lake and bought one that featured the willow in soft shades of green.

"This is beautiful," she told the young man. "I love this part of the lake, and now I'll always have it with me."

"My mom painted that," he said. "I'll tell her what you said. She'll be real happy."

Donald snorted.

They went into Mother's Sewing Basket and looked at locally made quilts and coverlets. Penny found a crazy quilt in shades of yellow. "This would look great on my bed," she said. Brian grew pale at the thought and moved closer to her. "Cheap fabric," Donald said. "They're using polyester instead of cotton." The little old woman stitching by the window looked ready to cry, so Kate bought a peach-and-blue comforter for her apartment.

"I've never had a real patchwork quilt before," she told the old woman. "This will keep me warm all winter."

"It will that," the old woman said, and patted her hand.

Donald sneered.

They went into Cline's Dry Goods and found rows of cotton and flannel shirts in bright plaids, stacks of dark blue jeans, and piles of socks, white T-shirts, and underwear that Donald snickered at. They also found, to Penny's delight, a rack of cowboy hats.

Mrs. Cline came out from behind the counter to help her.

"You're so pretty, you'll look a treat in any of them, honey," she told Penny. "It's a real pleasure to see you try them on."

Penny beamed at her and tried on a blue one with golden feathers around the crown.

"All right," Brian said.

"It's you," Kate said, laughing. "You have to have it."

"You, too." Penny pulled her over to the rack. "You get one, too."

Mrs. Cline picked up a red hat with white beads. "Try this one," she urged Kate. "You'd be a picture in a red dress and this one."

Kate hesitated, and Penny shook her head. "No. That one." She pointed to a black hat with silver medallions around its crown.

"That's for a man, honey," Mrs. Cline said, but she got it down anyway.

Kate put it on and mugged with Penny in the mirror.

"We'll wear these tonight," Penny said, and Kate was about to tell her no, cowboy hats weren't her style, when Donald picked the hat off her head.

"One hundred and twenty-five dollars? That's ridiculous."

Kate saw Mrs. Cline color.

"I don't think so." Kate took the hat back from him, even though she did think so. "This is a high-quality hat. I'd have to pay a lot more for this in the city."

She put it on again and let it slide back so it framed her face. She looked a little bald with all her hair pulled into a chignon, so she took the pins out and let her hair fall free.

"All right," Penny said.

"*Now* it's worth one hundred and twenty-five dollars," Donald said gallantly.

If she wore braids, she could pretend she was Annie Oakley. She'd always wanted to be Annie Oakley. What was she going to do with a one-hundred-and-twenty-five-dollar cowboy hat?

She looked at Mrs. Cline, who looked at her and smiled.

"I'll take it," she said. "Penny's, too. My treat."

"Oh, Kate, really?"

"Really," Kate said.

They went into Dickerson's Snack Shop because Kate said she was tired of shopping. In truth, she was tired of spending money on things she really didn't want. It'd be just her luck that the next place they'd end up would be a car dealership, and she'd have to make up for Donald's big mouth by buying a '69 Chevy.

"Hi, folks." A round little woman came to the table, a pad in her hand. "What'll it be?"

"Hamburger and fries, lots of catsup," Penny said.

"Hamburger and fries, lots of catsup," Brian said, adoringly.

"Do you have anything broiled?" Donald asked.

"Mashed potatoes and gravy," Kate said, reading the menu. "You have mashed potatoes and gravy?"

"Sure do." The little woman beamed at her. "I make 'em myself."

"I love mashed potatoes and gravy," Kate said. "Real homemade mashed potatoes and gravy. Two orders, please."

The potatoes when they came were light and fluffy, the gravy dark and speckled with meat chunks and scrapings.

"I've died and gone to heaven," Kate said and the little woman laughed.

"Kate," Donald said loudly when she'd gone back behind the counter, "they're instant."

Kate looked horrified. "They can't be." She tasted

them. They were thick and rich, full of butter and real potato. "They're real."

"No place like this could afford the time to make real mashed potatoes," Donald told her. "They're instant."

Kate ignored him. The gravy was salty and thick, the potatoes creamy, the meat falling apart on her fork. Who needed men? She had this.

"Kate!" Donald was as outraged as if he'd read her mind.

"They're real." She scooped up another mound. A piece of meat fell off, and she raised her fork to spear it.

"Let me see." He thrust his hand over the plate just as she aimed the fork.

Later, she couldn't remember whether she'd had time to stop, or if Donald's trying to ruin her potatoes the way he'd ruined everything else had made her temporarily insane. Whatever the reason, she stabbed him with the sharp, narrow, old-fashioned fork and hit a vein in the back of his hand.

Donald screamed, and she shoved his hand away so he wouldn't get blood on her potatoes.

"I'm so sorry, Donald," she said and took another bite.

An hour later, Kate stopped by the cabin and dropped off the things she'd bought and then strolled back to the pool for a while. Two orders of Mrs. Dickerson's mashed potatoes had made her world a better place, even though Donald tried to make her leave after Mrs. Dickerson had wrapped his hand in gauze.

"I'm almost finished," she'd told him, "and you're not bleeding anymore."

He was standing at the bar when she sat down next to the pool, drinking with his left hand and ignoring her. Obviously he wasn't going to be making any passes at her tonight. *Just as well,* she told herself. *He'd probably tell me that my nightgown was polyester and that I'd faked my orgasm. And he'd have been wrong about the nightgown and right about the orgasm.*

Penny waved to her and she moved to the chair beside her. "Thank you for talking me into going into town today," she told Penny. "I had a very good time."

"Well, don't forget, we're going to Nancy's tonight, too," Penny said.

"Anything you say," Kate said and slouched down in her chair to enjoy the late afternoon.

Jake watched her slouch and then deliberately turned away. She didn't seem upset, but something had pretty clearly gone wrong that afternoon; for one thing, Donald the gnat was wearing a bandage. She must have done something to him. Jake grinned, wondering what he had done.

He felt somebody at his elbow and turned to see Kate.

"Soda," she said. "Any kind. I'm dying of thirst."

"Sure." Jake moved behind the bar. "So how did the plan go today?"

Kate glanced over at Donald who was glaring at her as he nursed his hand. "Not well. Why?"

"I was curious as to why old Donald was wearing a bandage. You were my first guess. What'd you do, bite him?"

"He should be so lucky," Kate said. "I stabbed him."

Jake handed her a drink. "Try not to injure anybody else, okay?"

"He deserved it," Kate said.

"I'm sure he did. But if you go around wounding every guy who deserves it, you'll be taking out most of the hotel."

"I'll behave," Kate said. "I'm not even going to be at the hotel tonight. Penny's taking me someplace called Nancy's."

"I'll warn Nancy," Jake said.

"Very funny," Kate said and walked back to her chair while Jake watched.

I'm really not attracted to her kind, Jake thought. *Which is a good thing, because if I was, I could be in deep trouble here.*

Penny knocked on Kate's door at seven. "Come on, Kate," she called. "Let's go." She was wearing white hoop earrings the size of bracelets, her new cowboy hat, and a neon-blue scoop-necked cotton-knit shift that stopped a good distance above her knees. She had exquisite knees.

Penny came in and sat on the bed and her dress rose above her thighs. She had great thighs, too. "You're going to love Nancy's. Everybody says it's the best—a real country bar. Everybody goes there."

"Right," Kate said. "I'm going. Just give me a minute."

What to wear was a problem. She really liked Penny, but going places with her was depressing. *No thighs or knees,* she told herself. *You can't compete.*

She pulled her white silk halter dress out of the closet. It was a little formal and draped a little low in the back for a bar, but it was also calf-length. She looked at Penny's thighs. This was the dress.

She put her hair back in the chignon and put on her gold hoops.

"You should leave your hair down," Penny told her. "It looks really good down."

"It's messy." Kate tucked a loose strand firmly behind her ear.

"Men like messy hair. They like to touch it."

Kate looked at Penny's hair, tumbling all over her shoulders. It was lovely.

"Not my style." She put in another bobby pin.

Penny sighed and followed her out to the car.

Surprisingly enough, Kate liked the bar. It was everything Penny had said—a real country bar. The light was dim, the tables were scarred wood, and a jukebox glowed neon as it moaned country and western to the crowd. In the background, Kate could hear the snick of pool balls and see people playing under hanging lights, and somewhere someone was playing pinball. A real bar. Not a fern in the place.

A good-looking redhead was tending the old oak bar, wiping down the thick white-veined marble top. Like the rest of the waitresses, she was wearing a well-filled black tank top and a pink vest. Unlike the rest of the waitresses, she was self-possessed and over thirty. Kate made a bet with herself that this was Nancy.

"White wine, please." Kate sat on the barstool in front of her, and the redhead poured her drink. Penny stood with her back to the bar, surveying the room.

"I'm Nancy," the redhead said. "You want anything, just holler my name. Everybody else around here does."

Kate smiled. "I'm Kate. And this is Penny."

"I love your bar," Penny said, turning around. "It's just too authentic."

"Thanks," Nancy said. "That's definitely the ambience we wanted."

Kate looked at her with more interest than before. "Exactly how do you achieve this authentic ambience?"

"Oh, it's not hard. We just hire a couple of guys in plaid shirts to come in and play pool and spit on the floor."

"You hired them?" Penny asked.

"It's a joke, Penny," Kate said.

"Actually, the guy in the blue plaid shirt back there is my husband."

Kate looked back to the pool table. The guy in the blue plaid was blond and stocky. He was staring sadly at the table where a big man in a cream-colored cowboy hat was knocking balls into the pockets with disheartening precision.

"Isn't that Jake?" Penny asked.

"You know Jake?" Nancy shook her head. "He's beating Ben at pool. They've been playing off and on for about five years now. Ben's never won once."

"Why does he keep playing?" Kate asked.

"He says he's getting better."

"Well, you have to admire a man who doesn't quit."

"Jake says he's getting worse."

"Jake's dreamy," Penny said.

"Go tell him," Nancy said. "Maybe you'll distract him and Ben will win."

"Maybe later," Penny said. "We want to scope out the action. Right, Kate?"

"What do you want to drink, Penny?" Kate asked hastily. "I'll buy."

"Strawberry daiquiri," Penny said.

Nancy sighed.

"How about a beer?" Kate suggested. "Men in places like this love women who drink beer."

"Are you sure?"

"Did you ever see *Urban Cowboy*?"

"No," Penny said. "Beer, please."

"Thank you," Nancy said to Kate and went to get Penny's beer.

Over by the pool table, Ben looked up. "Check out the talent at the bar."

Jake glanced over his shoulder and stopped for a moment to stare. Then he turned back to the table. "The one in white is Kate."

"The killer?" Ben took a longer look. "That's some dress."

"Yep," Jake said. "I think you just lost this game, son."

Ben looked at him skeptically. "You said she was a nice kid."

"She is." Jake studied the table. "Aside from the damage she does to her dates."

He leaned over to take his shot, and Ben looked at him and shook his head. "That is no kid."

Jake pocketed the last ball. "No, but that is the game. You got time for another?"

"Hell, yes. My winning streak is about to start." Ben looked back at Kate. "She's not a real blonde."

"The hell she isn't."

"Twenty bucks says she isn't."

Jake looked at him in disgust. "And how do you propose we settle the bet?"

"I propose you find out," Ben said, grinning.

"Find out for yourself." Jake moved around the table to rack the balls. "But make sure I get the twenty from your estate. Death is no reason not to pay off your bets."

"This is a wonderful place, Penny," Kate said. "Thank you for bringing me. In fact, I like it so much, I'm going to buy the next round, too."

"Oh, shoot," Penny said. "We won't have to buy any more beers. That's what guys are for. Look at that guy in the black Stetson."

The guy in the Stetson was ersatz cowboy, right down to his spurs. Expensive ersatz cowboy. He was probably a dentist from Detroit. Still, if Penny liked him, Kate wasn't going to be a snob. "He's very attractive, Penny."

"He's smiling at us." Penny smiled back. The dentist ambled over.

"Howdy, little lady." He touched the brim of his hat. "Could I buy you a drink?"

"Sure could," Penny said. "This is my friend, Kate."

"Just leaving." Kate backed away a few seats, taking her wine with her. The dentist smiled his appreciation.

Why is it, Kate thought as she backed up, *that Jake and Penny can look honestly charming in their cowboy hats and yet this man looks like such a loser? And those spurs. Those spurs would make me very nervous.*

She stopped with a bump when she backed into someone. She turned to apologize and got a good look at the man she'd bumped—he was tall, rangy, blond, and devastatingly good-looking.

Hello, she thought. He wasn't exactly part of her plan, but then her plan was obviously not working anyway.

"Lemme buy you a drink, honey," he slurred, grabbing her arm.

The moment of her temptation was gone. She didn't like grabbers, especially drunk grabbers.

"Thanks but no thanks." She smiled sweetly and tried to move away from him, but he blocked her way, holding on to her.

"Back off, Brad," Nancy said from behind the bar. "She's not interested."

"She will be. Just got to give her a little time." Brad tried to kiss her but Kate ducked and all he caught was her ear. From the corner of her eye, she saw Nancy wave to somebody, and then she concentrated on getting away from Brad.

Across the room, Ben looked up at Nancy's wave and saw the minidrama unfolding at the bar.

"Uh-oh," he said. "Brad's putting the moves on your kid. Want to go save her?"

Jake looked up. "No." He sighed and put his cue down. "But I'll go save Brad. He's kind of obnoxious, but he doesn't deserve what Kate will do to him."

Six

"I'm warning you," Kate told Brad. "Let go of me or you'll be scarred for life."

"I like 'em spunky." Brad pulled her close again.

"Well, Brad, how's it goin'?"

Kate turned around and Ben was there, smiling at them, with Jake behind him.

"You don't want to mess with her, Brad," Jake said. "Trust me on this one."

"I saw her first." Brad shoved Kate behind him.

"I think the lady wants to go home, " Nancy said.

"She can go home with me," Brad said.

"I don't think so, boy." Ben took a step forward.

Brad moved into karate position, bunching his fists and glaring at the two men.

Jake sighed. "You've been watching TV again, haven't you, Brad?"

Kate could feel Brad tense. "Oh, hell," she said. She picked up a long-necked beer bottle from the bar and broke it over Brad's head, and Jake supported his weight as he sagged.

"You had to do it, didn't you?" Jake said to Kate.

"He was going to hit you," Kate said. "I saved you, you big ingrate."

"Where's the blonde?" Brad asked dazedly.

"I don't think she's really your kind of girl, Brad."

Jake helped him into a chair at the nearest table. "Those tough blondes, they'll hit you from behind with a bottle as soon as look at you."

"Very funny," Kate said.

Jake raised his eyebrows at her. "Well, you may have noticed that I've never turned my back on you."

"Anytime you want a job, lady," Nancy said, "you come to me."

"I'll keep it in mind," Kate said. "This is a great place. Allowing for the drunks and the wimpy bouncers."

"I'm not a bouncer." Jake looked indignant. "You a bouncer, Ben?"

"Hell no, I just like a fight. And if there's not gonna be one, I'm gonna go shoot pool. My winning streak's starting any minute here. You coming?"

"In a minute." Jake sat down at the bar. "Beer, please, Nan. And another drink for the lady with the broken bottle in her hand."

"Thank you," Kate said and joined him, putting the bottle neck on the counter.

"This is to show you that I'm grateful to you for saving me from Brad," Jake said. "I'm drinking beer, but of course you'll have juice."

"Beer, please." Kate ignored her wimpy white wine, and Nancy swiftly removed the evidence along with the broken bottle.

"I know I didn't save you from Brad," Kate said when the beers came. "I don't know what you were going to do, but you weren't worried."

"Oh, Brad's not a bad guy. He was just showing off for you."

"Very flattering."

"Oh, it is." Jake drank some of his beer. "Brad only makes passes at the best-looking women."

"Does he ever succeed?"

"Most of the time. I think that was his problem with you. He couldn't believe you were turning him down. Course he didn't know about your plan."

He grinned at her lazily, and Kate ignored the invitation to battle.

"You must have a resting pulse of about twelve," she said.

"I used to move a lot faster," he said. "It's age."

"No, it's not. I haven't figured out what it is, but it's not age."

"Well, when you figure it out, let me know so I can get it fixed." Jake took a drink. "You want me to drive you back to the cabin later?"

Kate frowned for a minute, assuming he'd changed his mind and was trying to pick her up, and then she realized he was asking if she was afraid to go home alone in the dark.

"No, thank you," she said. "I can handle it."

"I don't imagine there's much you can't handle," Jake agreed. "So how's the plan going, anyway?"

"Oh, I've retired it for the night," Kate said. "As I said this morning, it all seems rather stupid here."

"I'm relieved to hear it. I thought you might have looked on Brad as a potential candidate."

"I was trying not to be a snob," Kate said, remembering Donald. "He was friendly, so I was friendly."

"Well, your heart was in the right place. Just try to restrain your friendliness. You're giving the boys ideas."

Kate glared at him. "So this was my fault."

"No," Jake said. "But a little 'friendly' from you has a big impact. Particularly in that dress."

"What's wrong with this dress?"

"It has no back." Jake looked over her shoulder. "Not

that I'm complaining. We're just not used to seeing that much naked flesh in these parts. Sort of starts a man's blood moving, if you know what I mean.''

Kate tried to look over her own shoulder. ''What are you talking about? This dress has a back. It's just draped.''

''Well, the drapes are open.''

''Listen…''

''Hey, I'm not complaining. Just stop smiling at drunks.''

Kate controlled her temper with an effort. ''Thank you for the sound advice,'' she said finally. ''I shall certainly keep it in mind.''

Jake grinned. ''A man who didn't know better would tell you that you look real cute when you're mad. Fortunately, I know better.'' He finished his beer, tipped his hat to her, and ambled back to the pool tables.

''Has he always been like that?'' she asked Nancy when she came to clear their bottles.

''Like what?''

''Catatonic.''

Nancy snorted. ''He's not catatonic. That guy doesn't miss a thing.''

''Well, he sure moves slow.''

''Conserving energy. You interested?''

''No,'' Kate said. ''Not my type. I'm not his, either.''

''I don't think he has a type,'' Nancy said. ''He pretty much just likes everybody.''

Kate looked back and saw one of the college girls from the hotel, the pretty brunette, leaning on the pool table talking to Jake. He didn't seem to be annoyed by the attention. She was too young for him. Honestly. *Men.*

''Have another beer,'' Nancy said. ''On the house.''

Kate said, ''Thank you very much,'' and settled down

to talk to her for the rest of the night, ignoring the several hopeful men who offered to buy her drinks.

She and Nancy talked on through the evening as Nancy tended bar, comparing life stories and falling into the kind of friendship that women with the same outlook on life can form easily and permanently. It wasn't long before she told Nancy all about Jessie and the plan.

"I know it sounds stupid," Kate said.

"Oh, I don't know," Nancy said. "It beats sitting home and waiting for somebody to drop by."

"And I've made some big mistakes, too," Kate went on. "I was so fixated on 'successful' that I forgot to watch out for jerks. You should have seen my golf date."

"Is this the one that fibrillated on the hill course?" Nancy said. "I heard."

"And then there was the man I took shopping this afternoon." Kate shook her head. "I've never met such a snob."

"I heard about him, too," Nancy said. "I also heard you were very nice, and everyone wondered why you were with him."

"Everyone?" Kate said.

"It's a very small town," Nancy said. "They like you."

"Oh," Kate said, disconcerted. "I like them, too."

"Good," Nancy said. "Maybe you should start checking out the local guys instead of all these business types."

Kate shook her head. "I need someone who's comfortable in the city. I just have to find someone who's both successful and a human being."

"Well, keep your options open," Nancy said. "The right man for you may be right under your nose."

"Not with my luck," Kate said. "With my luck, the right man for me is fly-fishing in Alaska."

At ten, Penny left with the dentist, and Kate went around to the working side of the bar and helped Nancy, opening bottles and refilling pretzel dishes, slowly sipping beer with her in the lulls between customers. The wall behind the bar was filled with snapshots, and while Nancy served people, Kate studied them all, fascinated. As she looked at them, they became a composite of Toby's Corners for her. One was of two stocky women outside the bar smiling at the camera while they squinted into the sun, obviously friends who were pleased to be where they were together. Another was of a grizzled man in a beat-up hat holding up a huge trout, trying to look nonchalant, not completely hiding the grin that wanted to break through. There were several wedding pictures from several different decades, the brides' dresses changing with the times, the grooms' tuxes and seriously bewildered expressions remaining the same. And there were dozens of high-school pictures of teams and cheerleaders, teachers shaking hands with award winners, school plays, and graduating classes. The pictures were all of different people from different decades, but they were all alike, too. Kate studied them, trying to find what it was that tied them all together. It was the smiles, she finally decided. They all smiled like people who were where they belonged—comfortable smiles.

"Where did you get all of these?" she asked Nancy.

"People bring them in," Nancy said. "Some of them are family, some good friends. Jake's up there."

"Where?" Kate said, and Nancy pointed to a football player cradling a ball and looking menacingly at the camera.

He looked about twelve.

"What a baby," Kate said and laughed.

"Hey, he was a senior when that was taken," Nancy said, "and he was really good. He set a record that year for touchdowns in one season."

"And that would be how many?" Kate asked.

"Four," Nancy said. "We get whomped pretty regularly in football."

Kate laughed. "Does he still have the record?"

"Nope," Nancy said. "It fell four years later." She jerked a thumb at another snarling football player who looked even younger than twelve.

Kate squinted at the picture. "He looks familiar."

"That's Will," Nancy said. "He made five. Damn near killed himself to do it."

Kate raised her eyebrows. "A little rivalry there?"

Nancy shook her head. "Hero worship. Jake was everybody's hero." She frowned. "Sometimes I think that's part of what's wrong with him now."

"What's wrong with him?" Kate asked, confused.

"Well, he's not doing much with his life," Nancy said. "Around here that's not unusual in general, but it is for Jake. Jake was the one who was going places." She shook her head again. "Now Will's the one who's a wonder. Sometimes I think Jake likes it like that. Sometimes I think Jake got real tired of being the one to beat." She tilted her head and said thoughtfully, "You know, when Will got that last touchdown, Jake was in the stands cheering like crazy. A lot of people said that was real generous of him." She shook her head. "He just looked real relieved to me."

Kate looked back at Jake's picture and tried to reconcile the baby menace with the grown-up man. "I can't believe he's the same person," she said.

"Oh, he's not," Nancy said, moving toward another customer. "He's real different now."

After midnight, the bar was quieter and Sally and Thelma, Nancy's two waitresses, went home. Ben took over for Nancy so she and Kate could take a break, and they sat at the bar with their last drinks, mildly intoxicated and completely relaxed in each other's company.

"That's the first I've seen Ben work," Kate said. "What is he, a silent partner?"

Nancy shook her head. "He's an insurance agent. This is my bar. He just spends the evening here so we can be together."

"Oh, I thought you were running it together," Kate said, disappointed. "How did you come to own a bar by yourself?"

"My mom and aunt ran it before I did. About five years ago when the plant over in Tuttle closed, they decided to retire, and they gave it to me. I think they figured it was going to close along with everything else around here, and they just couldn't bear to see it end."

"And you changed the name to Nancy's?"

"Nope, it was always Nancy's. They opened it the year I was born and named it after me. I grew up in this bar. When I outgrew my playpen, they moved it out and put in the pinball machine."

"Beats day care."

"Absolutely."

"It's a great place," Kate said sincerely.

"Come back tomorrow night," Nancy said. "About eight. Wear a short black skirt, and I'll teach you how to tend bar."

"One of those useful skills you cannot learn in college." Kate sipped some more beer. "I'd love to." She looked at Nancy, smiling and serene across from her, and decided to get involved. "Listen, there's something you should know."

Nancy raised her eyebrows, and Kate hesitated and then plunged ahead.

"I've heard from a very reliable source that Will Templeton is planning to put in a country-style bar up at the hotel that will probably kill your business."

"You're crazy," Nancy said flatly. "Will would never do that. Who's your source?"

Kate sighed. "Will's fiancée, Valerie."

"Fiancé?" Nancy snorted. "In her dreams. Which is probably where this bar idea came from, too."

"You might want to talk to Will about it," Kate said. "Businessmen are capable of stabbing old friends in the back to get what they want." Her father came to mind. "You really should look into it."

"Listen," Nancy said. "You're saying this stuff because you don't understand. Valerie doesn't understand. When the factory in Tuttle went under, this town would have, too, if Will and Jake hadn't been here to bail us out. The only reason this town didn't die is that Jake gave Will the money to build that hotel and then they hired everybody and his brother to work there. They could have done everything a lot cheaper and a lot faster with skilled labor from the outside, but everything went through Toby's Corners first." Nancy shook her head. "If Will wanted to shut me down, he could do it without starting his own bar, anyway. When I took over, this place was a mess. I needed a second mortgage and the bank couldn't give me one because I had no collateral. So Will gave me one."

"Do you realize how vulnerable that makes you?" Kate asked. "A privately held mortgage?"

"I'm not vulnerable at all," Nancy said. "You're not

listening. Will holds the mortgage.'' She looked thoughtful. ''And I guess Jake. They're partners.''

''Still, Valerie...''

''You don't get it,'' Nancy said. ''We're family. All of Toby's Corners. Even if we're not related by blood, we're still family. Although most of us are related in some way,'' she added. ''Jake says that accounts for the slight weirdness of the population.''

''So how's the bar doing?'' Kate asked.

Nancy shrugged. ''Could be better. We're getting along. Toby's Corners likes us.''

''You could be pulling in more of the clientele from the resort,'' Kate said. ''Valerie is absolutely right about that. And those people have money.'' She looked around the cozy room. ''They'd pay premium prices for this ambience, spit and all.''

Nancy shook her head. ''We'd have to clean the place up, build on, buy in bigger quantities, all that business stuff. I'm not a businesswoman. I just like selling drinks and talking to people.''

Kate sipped her beer and thought about the situation. It was harder than usual because the beer was making her head swim, but she knew what she had to do. ''I'm a businesswoman,'' she said. ''Let me help you.''

''What?''

''You can make this place profitable without too much trouble,'' Kate said. ''For one thing, your prices are too low. You can't be selling your drinks at much above cost.''

''Kate, people in Toby's Corners don't have a lot of money.''

''Then charge the resort people more. Tell the town people there's a frequent drinker's discount if they show up at least once a week for a month. You have to build up some capital, invest in this place, and then refinance those mortgages.''

''Kate, I told you—''

''I know, I know, Will won't foreclose. But I think you're underestimating Valerie.'' Kate struggled to concentrate. ''First, work on a plan to expand. When you've got that, find a silent partner to pump some money in here in return for a share of the profits. Although...'' Kate slowed to consider. ''Actually, you'd be better off finding some MBA who needs a hobby. You could use a business partner.''

''No, thank you,'' Nancy said. ''This is my bar.''

''Okay,'' Kate said. ''I can understand that. Find a silent partner, but make it a formal, legal partnership, no more handshake mortgages with guys who are sleeping with barracudas.''

Nancy shook her head, but she looked thoughtful as she sipped her beer. ''And you could make this business plan?''

''It's what I do,'' Kate said. ''Usually I ask for an obscene fee, but I'll do it for you for free drinks for the rest of my life.''

''Deal,'' Nancy said suddenly, holding out her hand. ''Let's see the plan first. Then I'll decide.''

''Fair enough,'' Kate said, taking her hand. ''I'm going to enjoy this. I've never rescued a bar before.''

''Why does the sight of the two of you shaking hands make me nervous?'' Jake said from behind them.

''Because you're a wimp,'' Kate said, rolling her head back unsteadily.

''Never give this woman booze,'' Jake said to Nancy. ''She's not a drinker.''

''Don't pick on my pal,'' Nancy said, getting up to go

help Ben. "We've got big plans. Watch the bar while Ben and I do the register, will you?"

"Sure," Jake said.

"I think I'll go back to the cabins now." Kate slid unsteadily off her stool.

"You can't hold your beer, kid." Jake moved in close to support her. "I'd give up drinking the stuff if I were you. I'll drive you home."

"I'm perfectly capable of driving home."

This was so blatantly untrue that they both ignored it, and she sat back down.

"Who's gonna get us a couple more beers?" a guy at the end of the counter called.

"Coming right up." Jake went around to the other side of the bar to serve them.

"One for me, too, please," Kate said.

"You bet." Jake poured her a cup of coffee.

"You are no fun."

"I'm just trying to make sure your liver lasts until you get back to the city."

"My liver is in incredible shape."

"*Was* in incredible shape. You've pickled it since the last time you looked."

He went to serve the others and she sipped her coffee, watching him. He said, "Last drinks, boys," and gave one of the men a beer and the other one coffee.

"I wanted a beer," the man snarled.

"I know you did," Jake said. "It's a damn shame."

"Yeah," the guy said sadly. He sipped his coffee.

"How do you do that?" Kate asked Jake when he came back.

"What?"

"All these tough guys get ready to bash you and then they don't."

"You mean Henry? Henry McCrum wouldn't hurt anybody." He picked up a glass from a tray under the bar and began to polish it. "Henry's my old biology teacher. In fact he still teaches. Great guy, Henry. His wife, Millie, runs the bakery."

"He's a teacher and he drinks?"

"That's why he drinks. The man's been teaching biology to teenagers for twenty-eight years. It's a miracle he's sane. Sober would be too much to ask."

"And the other man?"

Jake glanced over. "That's Early. He's my uncle, and he's walking home."

Kate shook her head, marveling. "Do you know everybody around here?"

"Mostly. I grew up here."

"And then you moved to the city."

"Yep."

"And then you came back here and saved Toby's Corners."

Jake scowled at her. "I did not. I told you before, Will did. Who fed you that garbage?"

"Nancy," Kate said. "She's offered me a job. She's going to teach me to be a barmaid."

"You'll drink the profits."

"I will not."

"Kid, I've only known you two days and I've seen you plastered three times." He shook his head. "A bar would not be a good career move for you."

"Twice." Kate held up two fingers. "You've seen me plastered twice. I tried to get drunk at the luau, but it didn't work. I was perfectly sober when I pushed Lance into the pool. I'd do it again in a minute, too."

"Well, it's good to know you don't have any regrets."

"You make it sound like I'm a lush. This is only the second time I've been drunk in years."

"And I got to be with you both times."

"Sorry."

"It's okay. Just try not to pass out on me before I get you into bed."

Kate dropped her coffee cup.

"Let me rephrase that," he said, wiping up the spill. "Hauling your unconscious body into your cabin and dumping it on your bed is work for a younger man than I."

"I'm not that heavy."

"As a dead weight, you are."

"Forgive me." Kate drew herself up from the bar with dignity. "I will certainly stay conscious."

"Good. Hold that thought."

Jake went off to take Henry and Early's money.

"So you've got a mortgage on Nancy's bar," Kate said when he came back.

Jake winced. "Did she show you her underwear, too?"

"What are you talking about?" Kate asked.

"Well, she seems to have spilled her guts about everything else."

"She was just explaining to me that if you wanted to close this bar, you could foreclose on the mortgage."

"Why would I want to close this bar?" Jake asked, bewildered.

"So you can open one at the resort," Kate said.

"Oh, right." Jake nodded. "The Valerie angle. You can forget that. It's not happening."

"Valerie," Kate said, shaking her head. "She seems to think we're two of a kind. She wants me for a role model. Do you think I'm like Valerie?"

"No," Jake said. "You're not at all alike."

Kate closed her eyes. "Thank you," she said. "I would really have hated it if you'd thought we were alike."

Jake looked thoughtful. "So you told Nancy about Valerie's idea?"

"Penny said we should warn her. I thought we should stay out of it, but then I met Nancy, and, well, you know…"

"I know. Is Nancy worried?"

"No. She thinks you and Will are Santa Claus."

Jake grinned. "And what do you think?"

Kate looked at him. "I don't know Will at all, but you are definitely not Santa Claus. I don't know what you are. Disturbing, I guess. But I trust you. Nancy's right. She's safe. But, boy, somebody'd better stop Valerie."

"Oh, somebody will," Jake said mildly. "What do you mean, disturbing?"

"I don't know," Kate said, studying him. "I haven't got it figured out yet. Don't I disturb you?"

"Constantly," Jake said. "Drunks make me nervous."

"You're ducking the question," Kate said. "But I'm so tired, I don't care. Say good-night, Gracie, and take me home."

Jake saw her to the door and left. Nice man. Kate stripped off her clothes. She had pajamas somewhere, but they sounded like too much effort. She fell naked into the bed and it creaked under her. Nice sound. She crawled under the covers and curled up to sleep.

She'd had a wonderful time tonight at the bar. They were all such good people. And she was really looking forward to helping Nancy with the bar. That could be a lot of fun. A small business, not a big corporation. Running everything herself. Maybe she'd buy a bar when she got home.

She tried to picture herself with a little neighborhood bar, and it looked wonderful until her father walked in and sneered at it, the way Donald had sneered at Toby's Corners all day. They were wrong, but she knew that it mattered to her. She had to work at something she could be proud of. *Come on, Kate,* she told herself. *Back to your plan. You're wasting time hanging out with Jake. Tomorrow you're going to get serious about finding a man you can build a successful business with.*

That wasn't particularly appealing so she added, *And tomorrow you're going to save Nancy's bar.* She closed her eyes and smiled to herself and when she opened them again it was very early morning, the sun coming weakly through the window as it crept its way into the sky. *I feel so good here,* she thought. *I can do anything here. I can even possibly save a bar bare-handed.*

She thought of how proud Jessie would be of her, and then of how proud Jake would be, although he'd never tell her so, and Jake made her think of the lake, and then she remembered Jessie, saying that somebody exciting would swim in the nude. This early, the lake would be deserted and cool, so cool. The water would slide over her like silk.

I'm exciting, she thought. *So there, Jessie.*

She pulled on a cotton shift and left the cabin to walk down the path to the lake.

It was cold in the woods, and she shivered a little. She breathed in the smell of the woods and the breeze and the lake, smelling the water even before she saw it.

It was even more beautiful in the early morning, like rippled glass.

This was it. She took a deep breath and then kicked

off her sandals and pulled off her shift and went naked into the water as if going to a lover.

It was cold, but she walked into the water steadily, feeling her skin tighten and the muscles in her stomach contract.

When she was hip-deep, she dived in.

The water broke over her head, and she twisted in the cold, reveling in the feel of the water on her body as her muscles tensed. She came to the surface and stretched out her arms as she trod water, feeling the cool early-morning sun on her face, and then dived and swam again and again, as free as if she were ten years old, as alive as if she'd been making love. She never wanted to put on clothes again.

After half an hour, she turned to swim back to shore and saw Jake sitting by her clothes. At least she figured it was Jake. It was certainly his hat.

She swam in to the shore until she could almost stand shoulder-deep in the water. He just sat there, his forearms on his knees, his hands dangling in front of him, watching her tread water.

"Hello," she said.

"Morning," he said, grinning at her.

Go away, she thought, but she smiled back, trying to act unconcerned. "Did you come to watch?"

"No. I came to swim."

"Well, come on in." She gestured behind her. "There's plenty of room."

"Well, now, I don't know." He pushed his hat back a little farther on his head. "Are you naked?"

"Yes."

"Then there's not plenty of room." He shook his head. "I'll go in when you come out."

Kate almost asked him to put his hat over his eyes.

She knew he'd do it, but if she was going to swim in the nude, she should have the courage of her convictions. After all, it was just Jake.

On the other hand, even if it was just Jake, she was still embarrassed for him to see her naked.

While she pondered, he watched her, laughter in his eyes.

The hell with you, she thought. *Laugh at this, buddy.* "All right," she said. "The lake is yours."

She swam toward him until the water was waist deep, and then walked out.

Jake didn't move. In fact, he seemed frozen. She walked up beside him and bent to pick up her T-shirt. He was only inches away from her, and he turned and watched her as she bent. Then she straightened and arched her back to pull the shift over her head. The cotton stuck to the water on her body and it took a lot longer than she liked before she finally got it pulled over her hips.

"Well, you've certainly improved my morning," Jake said.

"Anything to oblige." Kate picked up her towel and scuffed on her sandals. "Have a nice swim," she said and walked into the woods, her heart beating like mad.

Jake sat there for a while after she'd gone, stunned.

She'd looked so funny in the lake, biting her lip, trying to figure out what to do, and then, just when he'd been about to turn his back, she'd gotten that look in her eye and come walking out of the lake toward him.

Ben was right. She was no kid.

He'd felt like a rabbit caught in headlights. He hadn't been able to take his eyes off her body, round and full and taut with the cold. She'd strolled out of the lake like a goddess, and if it had taken one more second for her to pull that cotton thing on, he'd have reached for her.

He closed his eyes. Narrow escape. In fact, it would be a good idea to stay away from Kate since she was turning out to be the most confusing woman he'd ever known. He'd thought she was just another empty suit, but out on the lake she was the best company he'd ever had. He'd thought she was a snob, but she defended Nancy against Valerie. He'd thought she was cold, but she swam naked in the lake and, from the expression on her face, loved it. He'd thought she was an attractive woman, but lately her beauty was beginning to take on mythic proportions in his dreams.

And what he'd seen today was not going to help matters.

Sighing, he took off his clothes and went into the lake. It felt like a cold shower, which was just what he needed anyway.

When Kate got back to the cabin, she slammed the door behind her, her face burning with embarrassment. She'd done it.

The only problem was, now she had to face him sometime again.

The more she thought about it, the braver she felt. Big deal. He'd seen her naked. It was her choice. And he probably didn't give a damn. And, the sooner she faced him, the sooner she'd stop dreading it. She'd just act like nothing happened. No big deal.

In fact, the more she thought about it, the prouder she was of herself for being so free, so brave. Jessie would have loved it.

She had steak and eggs and home fries for breakfast

Seven

"Nice hat" was all Jake said when he saw her, and Kate breathed a tiny sigh of relief. *Still buddies,* she thought. *I'd have missed him.* She got in the boat, and he rowed over to the willow.

They took off their shirts, set their poles and then leaned back. Their legs stretched out in the boat companionably next to each other, and Kate no longer worried about touching him, absentmindedly enjoying the warmth of his skin next to hers, as she pulled out her book and began to read.

Jake watched her read. He was glad she'd come back because he would have missed her. There really wasn't any problem because as attractive as Kate was, she'd made it clear that he was not part of her plan. There was no danger. And now that she was back, he felt comfortable again. He hadn't lost anything by seeing her naked except for the few brain cells he'd burned out looking directly at her breasts.

He looked up into the willow and listened to the water lap against the boat. *It's a good life,* he thought and pulled his hat over his eyes and slept.

Half an hour later, Kate was deep in her book and didn't notice the tug on Jake's line until the pole was nearly bent to the water.

"Jake!" she called, and when he didn't answer, she swatted his leg with her foot.

He woke up grumpy.

"What?"

"There's something on your line."

He tilted his hat back and then sat up fast, grabbing the pole before it flipped into the water.

"Damn," he said, and fought the fish. It was a big one, and it broke the water battling, flapping water all over him as he ducked and tried to grab it.

Kate reclined in her end of the boat and watched Jake fight the good fight while she ate her second apple.

Finally, drenched and exasperated, he got the fish off the hook and threw it back in the lake. He sat looking at her, his forearms on his knees, his hands dangling in front of him, water dripping off his chest, arms and hands.

"You were a great help," he said.

"If I'd known you were going to be this energetic," she said, "I wouldn't have brought you." She tossed her apple core back over her head into the lake. "Now cut the hook off your line. The fish around here are positively suicidal."

Jake shook his head at her stupidity. "What does a fish have to be depressed about?"

"Fine." Kate waved her hand at him. "Slap yourself in the face with a fish again." She leaned back in the boat and picked up her book. "Just make sure you let me know. I don't want to miss it."

A few moments later she heard the soft snick of his knife cutting through the line, and she grinned to herself.

"Give me an apple," Jake said and she put her book down and tossed him one. He lay back in his end of the boat and bit into it.

"Where'd you get the hat?" he asked.

"Cline's."

"It looks really good on you."

"I know. I think it's sexy."

He studied her critically for a while. "No," he said finally. "It's not sexy, but it looks good."

Kate smiled smugly. "Well, I'm counting on it being sexy. I have a date this afternoon."

"Oh, Lord." Jake closed his eyes. "Who are you going to destroy now?"

"I beg your pardon?"

"The hotel would appreciate it if you'd just throw back the men you don't like without maiming them."

"I haven't maimed anyone."

"You almost drowned Lance, you scared Peter into heart palpitations, you stabbed Donald with a fork, and you hit Brad over the head with a bottle." Jake shook his head. "And they still ask you out."

"Lance asked for it, Peter was cheating, Donald was an accident, and, I might point out, I hit Brad to save you—an act I have regretted ever since."

"They ask you out, but they don't keep you. Has any guy actually finished a date with you?"

Kate sat up, outraged. "Listen, I've had *affairs* with men."

Jake snorted. "So you've said, but where are they now?"

Kate glared at him. "Is there a point to this?"

Jake shrugged. "Just that it takes a brave man to spend time with you."

"You spend every morning with me."

"Yeah, but I make sure you stay in your end of the boat. If you try to get any closer, I'm going overboard."

"You're safe." Kate sniffed. "I never attack wimps in boats."

"I'm glad you have some standards. So, who's the doomed man today?"

"Eric Allingham," Kate said and waited for Jake to tell her that Allingham was a Nazi. When all he did was frown and take another bite of apple, she said, "Well?"

"Well, what?"

"Well, what's wrong with him?"

Jake shrugged. "Aside from the suicidal tendencies he must have if he's dating you, nothing that I know of. Seems like a really nice guy." He chomped into his apple again with more energy than was necessary.

"I think so, too," Kate said doubtfully.

"You sound real enthusiastic," Jake said.

"Well, after spending the morning watching you trout-wrestle, I find it hard to believe that Eric will be able to measure up in entertainment value," Kate said. "You're a hard act to follow."

Jake shook his head. "Today was special. Don't count on me slapping myself in the head with a fish whenever you get bored, because it's not going to happen."

"I've got a date tomorrow, too," Kate said. "My plan may actually be working."

"You can't be that dumb," Jake said.

Kate ignored him. "A really nice date."

"Okay," Jake said. "I'll bite. Who will the rescue squad be picking up tomorrow?"

"Rick Roberts, the environmentalist. We're hiking." When Jake didn't say anything, Kate asked, "Do you know him?"

"Yeah," Jake said, a trifle sourly. "Your taste is improving. He's a great guy."

"I'm glad you approve."

"I don't. Stay away from cliffs and busy roads." Jake pulled his hat over his eyes. "Watch where you're going.

Do not antagonize the wildlife. In fact, my advice is stay in the hotel. You're due to give someone some serious trouble here shortly. It might be a good idea to stay within reaching distance of 911.''

''Very funny.'' Kate lay back and pulled her hat over her eyes. ''I don't know why you're so relaxed. I spend more time with you than anyone else. The law of averages says you're the next to go.''

''Not me.'' Jake yawned. ''I'm too old and too cautious to let you catch me napping.''

He drifted off and Kate heard his deep, even breathing. *I should tip you out of the boat,* she thought. *Too old and too cautious. As Jessie would say, what a crock.*

Then she fell asleep and they dozed together under the willow, rolling toward each other until their legs tangled as they slept.

At eleven, Kate woke Jake up when she went searching in the cooler for juice.

''You know, you used to be peaceful,'' he grumbled.

''I can't believe you were ever married,'' Kate said, as she cracked the can open. ''What did you do, make her stand in the corner all the time?'' She drank some juice.

''Tiffany was not the type to stand in corners,'' Jake said.

Kate spat her juice all over him as she laughed.

Jake sat up and glared at her. ''What the hell?''

''You married somebody named Tiffany?'' Kate said. ''I can't believe it.''

''At least I only have one mistake in my past,'' Jake pointed out as he mopped the juice off with her shirt. ''You've got Dopey, Grumpy, and Sleazy.''

''Paul, Derek, and Terence,'' Kate said.

Jake's laugh held a lot of contempt. "Good Lord, woman, where did you find them? Twits 'R' Us?"

"They were very nice men," Kate lied. "Did Tiffany dot the *i* with a little heart?"

"Tiffany was an assistant district attorney," Jake said. "Don't be such a snob."

"If Tiffany was so hot," Kate shot back, stung, "why aren't you still with her?"

"Because I wasn't hot," Jake said.

"Oh," Kate said. "I'm sorry."

"No, dummy," Jake said, patiently. "I didn't mean she dumped me. She was going places I didn't want to go. We parted by mutual consent."

"Oh," Kate said again. "That must be nice."

"It was hell." Jake frowned at her. "Nice? Are you nuts?"

"No." Kate frowned back. "I've just never parted with anyone by mutual consent. I've always had to escape while someone was holding on to my ankle."

"If they'd been dating you, I can't believe there was enough life left in them to keep a grip on you," Jake said.

"They weren't really gripping me," Kate said, staring off into space. "They just hated letting go of the money."

Jake leaned forward to get a beer. "Just how much money are we talking about, here?" he asked, not really caring.

Kate looked up. "Oh, I don't have that much. But my father does."

Jake frowned as he drank. "Should I have heard of your father?"

"Bertram Svenson?"

"Oh, hell," Jake said. "I met him once."

"I'm sorry," Kate said.

"No, no," Jake said. "He was very…"

"It's all right."

"Very…forceful."

"He really hated Paul, Derek, and Terence," Kate said.

"He looked like he was a sensible man," Jake said. "Is that why you dumped them?"

"No," Kate said. "I hated them, too."

Jake drank some more beer. "Uh, there's no really tactful way of asking this, so I'll just ask. Why did you get engaged to them if you hated them?"

"I didn't hate them until after I was engaged to them," Kate said. "It always took me a while to figure out that they were more interested in the money than in me."

"They couldn't have been that dumb," Jake said, and Kate looked up, surprised. "Well, you're not my type, but no man in his right mind would look at you and say, 'All this woman's got going for her is money.' They were interested in you, too."

"Not really," Kate said. "They were interested in how good I'd look standing beside them, at best. They didn't know me."

"Their loss," Jake said.

"Thank you." Kate bit her lip. "Tiffany couldn't have been too bright, either, to let you get away."

"Tiffany was very bright," Jake said. "And she didn't let me get away. She opened the door and I ran."

"It was that bad?" Kate shook her head. "I can't imagine you running."

"Oh, very funny," Jake said. "I was younger then."

"I still can't imagine you having that much energy."

"Listen, if I got in the same situation today, I'd find that much energy again." Jake shook his head and finished his beer. "Damn woman thought I was a mind reader. She kept hinting at things, and I'd miss 'em, and then all hell would break loose. Plus she had this idea that I was some sort of tycoon, and that we'd be building this empire together. By the time I figured out what she wanted, I'd spent six months getting bitched at every time I turned around."

Kate looked surprised. "You were only married six months?"

"With Tiffany," Jake said, "six months was plenty."

"Oh." Kate tried to understand. "And you didn't notice this plan of hers before you got married?"

"The only thing I noticed," Jake said, "was that she had a great body and we were terrific in bed."

"Oh." Kate felt depressed. "And that wore off."

"Fast," Jake said.

"Oh." She tried again. "And this was how long ago?"

Jake frowned, trying to count back. "About seven years. Maybe eight. What year is it?"

"And you're still avoiding women?" Kate's sympathy evaporated. "At least I keep trying."

Jake snorted. "Yeah, and look who you keep trying with. At least I'm not dating Tiffany clones and trying to kill them to get even."

"I'm not trying to kill them," Kate said. "I'm just trying to find someone, and they keep self-destructing."

"Maybe you should stop trying to find someone," Jake said, settling back.

"No!" Kate said, surprising herself with her own force. "I'm tired of being alone. I want someone to talk to at night. Someone to laugh with. Someone to…"

Jake raised his eyebrows. "What?"

"Nothing."

They both observed a polite silence while they thought

about the nothing, Jake picking up another apple from her bag. After a while, he changed the subject. "So what're you doing tonight after you've finished off Allingham?"

"I'm going to Nancy's. She's going to teach me to bartend."

"Good." Jake bit off another chunk of apple. "I think it's important for a woman to have a career."

"That's real liberated of you, Jake."

"Yeah. I'm a nineties kind of guy." He looked up at the sun and sighed. "Time to go back in." He sat up, took the last bite of apple and threw the core in the lake, and stowed the cooler away so he could row. "Tell you what. Come on back to the pool table when you're done with Nancy, and I'll teach you to shoot pool like a real hustler."

"All right," Kate said, surprised. "I've never played pool."

"Good. We'll play for money."

Jake put the poles in the boat and untied the line from the tree. As he reached for the oars, he asked, "How come I always have to row?"

"'Cause I'm a fifties kind of gal," Kate said, and tipped her hat down over her face.

When Kate looked back on that afternoon with Eric Allingham, there was a certain inevitability to the whole thing, as if she was caught up by forces beyond her control.

Eric was tall, distinguished, discerning, successful, honest, kind, considerate, clean, brave, and reverent. He was also a little boring, but Kate stomped on the part of her that noticed that. He was a good man. That should be enough. He was patient with her and gentle with the horses. Under his tutelage, she found herself in the saddle of a sleepy mare, clutching the reins with much less fear than she would have been if he hadn't been beside her.

"This is very nice of you," she said to him.

"My pleasure," he told her and he really seemed to mean it.

This is a very nice man, she thought. *At last, my plan is working.*

Then the mare kicked him in the knee, and he went down without a sound.

"Whatever you do," she told Will when he brought the doctor, "don't tell Jake."

All afternoon, Jake felt vaguely uneasy about Kate's date with Eric Allingham. He couldn't figure out why. Allingham was a very nice guy. After the string of losers Kate had been out with, Allingham would be a pleasant surprise. He might even be the key to her stupid plan. For some reason, that thought did not cheer him.

The sight of the rescue squad turning down the lane toward the stables did, though. Of course, the squad could be going down there for somebody else, he reasoned, but if he knew Kate, Allingham was in need of medical attention.

And, he thought complacently, *I know Kate.*

After an afternoon in the emergency ward, Kate tried to forget about Eric and concentrate instead on getting ready to be a barmaid. It had seemed like a wonderful idea the night before, but eighteen hours later, without the lubricating power of beer, she felt uneasy.

The phone rang and she picked it up.

"Hello?"

"So are you engaged yet?"

"Jessie, it's Tuesday. I've only been here four days. I am not engaged yet. Don't you have anything better to do than call for hourly updates?"

"No," Jessie said. "What's up? How were the new guys?"

"The new guys?" Kate started to laugh. "Not good." Then she remembered Eric and stopped laughing. "Not good at all."

"Did you kill another one?"

"Stop it. You sound just like Jake."

"Oh, yeah, Jake. How's old Jake?"

"Obnoxious. How did the Dershowitzes like their cake?"

"They loved it. So tell me about Jake."

"Why?" Kate stretched out on the bed and prepared to humor Jessie.

"Because I think he sounds interesting," Jessie said.

"Well, he's not. But I am. You'd be very proud of some of the things I've done."

"Like what?" Jessie said skeptically.

"Well, I'm saving a bar."

"Oh, good," Jessie said. "We need more of those."

"No, this is a little neighborhood bar. One owner, with mortgages. You'd like her. Her name's Nancy."

"Just like the good old days," Jessie said and Kate could tell from her voice that she was pleased. "So you're doing a business plan, right?"

"Right. I knew you'd be happy."

"Why don't you date the banker who holds the mortgages?" Jessie suggested. "Then when you've got him on his knees pleading for his life, you could bargain for the papers."

"There is no banker," Kate said.

Jessie waited, and when Kate didn't say anything, she

said, "So who does have the mortgages? Come on, spill it."

"Jake," Kate said.

"Jake?" Jessie sounded confused. "A handyman-banker?"

"He's not exactly a handyman," Kate said. "Anyway, I'm going back to Nancy's tonight and pick up the books, and then she's going to teach me to be a barmaid."

"A barmaid." Jessie started to laugh. "That's terrific. A real career for a change."

"I think it will be fun," Kate protested.

"Good," Jessie said. "I can't remember the last time you did something just for fun. Everything with you is business."

"Not everything," Kate said. "I went skinny-dipping this morning."

"You're kidding." Jessie sounded impressed. "Totally nude?"

"Totally. It was lovely."

"Where'd you find a private place down there? I figured every square inch would be crawling with guests."

"There's a little lake that's very secluded," Kate said. "And I got up very early."

"So you were all alone," Jessie said dreamily. "I may come down there yet." When Kate didn't say anything, she added, "You were all alone?"

"Well, in the beginning," Kate said, hating where the conversation was going. "So what cake are you working on now?"

"What do you mean, 'in the beginning'?"

"Nothing. You are working on a cake, right?"

"Right. A wedding. So what happened?"

"Nothing happened. Whose wedding?"

"Kate."

Kate sighed. "I stayed out too long. Jake was on the shore when I came in."

Jessie started to laugh. "I have got to meet Jake. So how did you get out of it? No, wait, wait. I know. You made him turn his back, and he did because he's a gentleman."

"No, I didn't," Kate said, stung. "I just walked out of the lake, put on my shift, and went back to the cabin."

"You let some guy see you in the nude?" Jessie shrieked.

"Well, it's not as if no man had ever seen me naked before," Kate said.

"Full frontal nudity in broad daylight with a complete stranger?"

"Jessie, it was just Jake."

"Just Jake." Jessie was silent for a minute. "Did he say anything?"

"Yes," Kate said. "He said that I'd improved his morning. Now tell me about the cake."

Jessie started to laugh again. "How are you ever going to face this guy again?"

"I spent the rest of the morning on the lake with him," Kate said. "He's teaching me to play pool tonight. He's just a friend. That's all. Not part of the plan. But speaking of the plan, I went horseback riding with a very nice man this afternoon who may be perfect."

"You were on a horse?"

"Certainly," Kate said. "Eric showed me how. He was very patient."

"You went horseback riding?"

"Well, not exactly." When Jessie didn't say anything, Kate sighed and went on. "The horse kicked him in the knee, so we had to go to the emergency room—" She stopped because Jessie was laughing again. "Stop it. He was a wonderful man."

"Well, he's not dead, just lame," Jessie said. "Tell me more about Jake."

"I'm not interested in Jake," Kate said.

"Well, I might be," Jessie said. "He sounds great. How old is he?"

"I don't know," Kate said, annoyed. "Late thirties, maybe."

"Married?"

"Divorced," Kate said. "From an assistant district attorney named Tiffany who was great in bed."

"My, my, my," Jessie said. "Tell me more."

"No," Kate said. "He's not your type. I have to go. I have to get ready to bartend. And then I have to call Eric and see how he's feeling because he has real potential for my plan. And tomorrow, I'm going out with an environmentalist named Rick, whom even Jake says is a great guy."

"Jake, again. Are you sure he's not my type?"

"Absolutely," Kate said.

"Does he have any brothers?"

"Will," Kate said. "He's younger than Jake, very good-looking, extremely nice, wears a suit like a *GQ* cover, runs the hotel almost by himself, and is considered a local hero by the town because he saved the place single-handed. Come on down. I'll introduce you."

"A suit? No thanks, but he sounds like the perfect guy for you," Jessie said. "You could run the hotel together."

"Will?" Kate thought about it. "No. He's darling, but he's not for me."

"Why not?"

"I don't know." Kate was annoyed again. "He's practically engaged to this barracuda named Valerie. And he's not... I don't know."

"He sounds like your plan in the flesh," Jessie said. "I'd go for it if I were you and if I were still committed to following an extremely dubious plan that I should have dumped days ago."

"This plan is going to work," Kate said. "Now I have to go. I'm bartending tonight."

"Call me tomorrow," Jessie said. "I want to know what happens with Ron."

"Rick."

"Whatever. And give Jake my love. Tell him I can't wait to meet him."

"I told you. He's not your type," Kate said and hung up to the sound of Jessie's laughter.

I don't know what she thinks is so funny, Kate thought, and then dismissed Jessie from her mind as she opened her suitcase to find something to wear.

Black underwear? She found some sheer stuff embroidered with pink and gold flowers. Classy. Her black straight skirt was calf-length, and on an impulse, she took her nail scissors and cut it off above the knee. She took down her hair, and then because her head looked sort of vulnerable under all those curls, she put on her black cowboy hat before she went out the door.

She stopped on the top step. Her car was gone. She'd left it at Nancy's the night before when she'd had too many beers to drive. Now what? Did she call Nancy? Walk? What?

After a little thought, she sat down on the top step to wait. He wasn't distinguished, discerning, or successful, but he was dependable. Jake, she knew, would remember she had no car and would come to get her.

* * *

At seven-thirty, Jake got into his car to go to Nancy's and found one of Kate's shoes in the front seat. Terrific. Her car was down at the bar. He sighed and drove to Kate's cabin, pretending an exasperation that he really wasn't feeling. When he pulled up in front, she was sitting on the cabin steps in a tight, short skirt, waving at him. She had very nice, very long legs, he noticed. She would be collecting some hefty tips. And probably a few hefty passes. He felt a faint concern, which he told himself was solely for the men of his town.

Kate got in and smiled at him. "I was getting ready to walk, but then I realized you'd show up and rescue me. I'm very grateful. And I'm giving up drinking forever so you won't have to bring me home."

"No problem," he said. "Just do me a favor and try not to make a date with anybody from town tonight. The population's pretty small as it is."

"Very funny," Kate said.

Jake grinned. "Speaking of you and men, what did you do to Allingham this afternoon?"

"Nothing," Kate said.

"I saw the rescue squad."

"The horse kicked him."

"You sure you left those three guys you were engaged to?" Jake said. "Have their bodies been found?"

"Just drive," Kate said.

Nancy handed her a tank top and vest as she came through the door. "You're a professional now. Here's the uniform."

When she put them on in the storeroom, the tank top was a little tighter than she would have chosen, the vest a little looser. Who cared? She was in Toby's Corners, and she was going to have fun.

"I feel like Debra Winger in *Urban Cowboy*," she told Nancy as she tilted her hat back. "Except taller, fatter, older, and blonde."

"Other than that, you're a dead ringer," Nancy agreed, handing her a tray with six beers on it. "The hat's a nice touch. Keep it on. This goes to the corner table at the front. Watch the guy in the bowling shirt. He has hands. Oh, and the records you wanted for the plan are in the back. You can take them back to the cabin with you for tonight, if you want."

"I want," Kate said. "I'm really looking forward to this. I love financial planning."

"I'd rather shoot myself in the foot," Nancy said. "But each to his own, I guess."

"Well, right now my own is being a barmaid," Kate said, checking her hat in the mirror. "I'm going to be great."

She felt great. Her hair was loose on her shoulders, her body round in the low-cut tank top, her face flushed from the heat and exercise. She would never have planned to look that way, but she found after her first embarrassment that being riotously feminine was intoxicating. She knew she looked good because of the way the men looked at her, a way she wasn't used to. She was used to cool, approving looks that evaluated her like she was an expensive piece of porcelain. The men at Nancy's looked at her like she was flesh and blood. It was disconcerting and fun. She felt powerful instead of possessed, appreciated instead of coveted. She tilted her hat back and smiled at everyone, practicing her own version of the friendly, mild flirting that Nancy used on every male she met; and the men were responsive to a flattering degree. The women, she found, were just plain friendly. She felt happy and curiously alive. The only plan she had in mind now was the one for Nancy's bar.

However, being a barmaid, Kate discovered, wasn't all bounce and smile. The bonuses were the friendly people, the cheerful atmosphere, the tips, and working with Nancy. The downside was the constant walking and the hands.

"Just move around them, honey," Thelma, one of the barmaids advised her. "If they connect, spill a little beer on them."

Sally, the other barmaid, pointed out the worst offenders. "Give them their drinks from across the table. They'll look down your bra, but they won't be able to reach you."

Nancy showed her how to mix drinks, draw beer, and work the register. Kate concentrated like she hadn't since college, learning not only the names of the drinks but the names of the customers and what they drank. When Jake's Uncle Early, a potbellied man in a stained shirt, came to the bar and said, "Another one, please," she said, "Gin," and poured.

Nancy was impressed. She was even more impressed when she realized that Kate could do it with anyone by their third drink.

"How'd you do that?" she asked.

"Mnemonics," Kate said. "It's the way I got through college. You make up a sentence that links the two words. You know, it's too Early for Gin."

Nancy shook her head. "Amazing."

"I think I've got the hang of it." Kate felt absurdly proud.

"I think so, too." Nancy handed her two beers. "Jake and Ben. They're due."

* * *

Kate threaded her way back to the pool table.

"Hey," she said, and they stood back for her.

Jake looked at her tank top as he took his beer, and then he looked away. "Nice outfit," he said. "Injured anybody lately?"

"Give it a rest," Kate said. "Not everyone is as big a wimp as you."

"Oh, almost forgot," Jake said and tipped her five bucks.

"What's this for?"

He picked up his cue and chalked it. "Helping me settle a bet with Ben."

"What bet?"

"Whether you were a real blonde or not."

The lake that morning. Kate blushed brick red and turned back to the bar. She stopped before she got there and walked back to him.

"Who won?" she asked.

Jake made his shot. "I did. Ben's a cynic."

By ten the bar was almost empty, so everybody saw Sally swerve to avoid Brad's hand, slip in some spilled beer, and sprain her ankle.

Jake looked at Kate. "I warned you," he said. "I pleaded with you not to maim any more of the population."

"Oh, please," she said. "This is my fault?"

"Okay, you're right." He put down his cue. "This one isn't your fault." He left to help Ben get Sally into Thelma's car.

Nancy waved her over. "That job offer is really serious now. Can you fill in for Sally for a couple of nights?"

"Sure," Kate said.

"Six to eleven, Wednesday and Thursday. If Sally's not back by Friday, six to one."

"Sounds good," Kate said and went to clear a table. *My feet hurt, but I like it here,* she thought. *I owe Jessie big for this one.*

Eight

By eleven, Kate's feet were beyond hurting and into agony.

She walked back to tell Jake their game was off for the night, that she simply couldn't stand up another moment, but when she got back to him, he smiled, and she wasn't tired anymore.

"This is the cue ball." He picked up the only white ball on the table. "Do not hit the cue ball into the pockets. That is bad."

Ben shook his head and moved away.

"You might want to stay," Jake said to him mildly. "Some of this stuff you haven't mastered yet."

"Don't play for money," Ben warned her as he left. "The guy's a shark."

"Okay, no white ball in the pockets," Kate said.

Jake put all the colored balls inside a triangular frame. "This is a rack. You rack the balls to start."

He had nice hands. Long fingers. She watched him pull the rack away and put the cue ball a little way from the point of the racked balls.

"To start the game, you have to break the racked balls." He crooked his finger at her. "Come here."

He put a cue in her hand. "Make a bridge," he said, showing her how. Then he moved the cue over her fingers. "The cue should slide over the bridge when you shoot."

"Got it." Kate concentrated on her bridge, making it as close to Jake's example as she could. "Now what?"

"Line up the cue with the cue ball."

"Right." Kate bent over the table, absentmindedly feeling her short tight skirt ride up on her thighs. She sighted down the cue so that the point was in the middle of the white ball.

"Now what?" she asked. He didn't say anything, and she looked around and found him looking at the back of her skirt and shaking his head.

"Jake?"

"Don't wear that skirt to play pool. Now I know how those other guys went. I almost had a heart attack myself."

"Very funny." She yanked her skirt down over her rear end and felt it part company with her tank top.

"Okay," he said. "Hit the cue ball and scatter the other balls on the table."

She bent over the table again, and took her shot, but the cue hit the table and bounced into the cue ball. "Sorry," she said.

"My fault." Jake racked the balls again. "I wasn't paying attention. Okay, hold the cue again."

She lined up the cue with the ball and he came up behind her. "Your cue's up too high. Flatten it out so it's parallel to the table."

She overcompensated.

"No. Bring the tip down a little lower."

She dipped it again.

"No," he said.

"Show me," she said, frustrated. "I don't see what you mean."

He bent over her, putting his hands on top of hers. "Like this."

Kate concentrated on getting the angle right, and then noticed that he'd frozen over her. "Jake?" she asked and then realized what he had realized—that he was wrapped around her, the warm length of him touching her back all the way down, his hands curled over hers. She froze, too.

He stood slowly. "Just hit the ball."

Jake taught her the rest of the basics standing far away across the table from her. The problem with this noble plan was that he could see down her tank top every time she bent to take a shot, and it clearly distracted him. Kate enjoyed it, just as she'd enjoyed the admiration of the other men in the bar. There was something intoxicating about seeing Jake flustered. She lifted her chin a little so he could see down her cleavage a little more clearly.

Jake sighed and moved to the side of the table.

"Great game," she said, when they quit an hour later.

"Oh, yeah," he said, heading for the bar. "I need a drink."

Kate went into the back room and came out with a sloppy stack of mismatched folders.

"What are you doing?" Jake asked.

"Saving the plantation from the Yankees who hold the mortgage," Kate said.

"Hey," Jake said, rescuing a folder as it slipped from the stack. "Watch your mouth, woman."

"All I know is, the bad guy always has a mustache," Kate said. "I haven't seen you twirl yours yet, but I fig-

ure it's only a matter of time. Night, Nancy, Ben. Thanks
for the pool lesson, Jake.''

"You can't twirl this kind of mustache," Jake said,
but she was already gone.

He turned to find Nancy grinning at him.

"That woman annoys me," he said, and followed Kate
out the door, forgetting his beer, only to see her car pull
out before he could stop her and defend his mustache.

Kate and Penny arrived back at the cabin at the same
time, Penny arm in arm with Mark this time.

"I meant to tell you, that was a great golf game the
other day," Mark told Kate, "although you probably
shouldn't have killed him."

"I didn't kill him." Kate tried to look innocent. "The
doctor said he could come back tomorrow."

"If you play him again, I'll caddie for free."

"Oh, no. I'm giving up golf. It's too dangerous." She
waved good-night to them as she went inside.

She could hear their voices as they sat on the steps,
laughing and talking together. For the first time, Kate
envied Penny. Mark was attractive, smart, and funny.

She didn't want Mark. But she sure wanted someone.
Stop it, she told herself. *Think about something you're
good at, like saving Nancy's bar.*

Kate worked on the books until two and then shoved
them and her legal pads full of notes to one side of the
bed before sinking down under the covers. The bar could
be made comfortably profitable with a few easy changes,
but it could be a gold mine only with massive infusions
of capital and major changes.

Major changes that Nancy wouldn't want to deal with.

But I would, she thought. *Give me that bar and I could...*

But she couldn't. First of all, the bar was Nancy's and she loved it and, Kate knew without a doubt, it was Nancy that made the bar work.

And besides, even if Nancy would sell, the bar wouldn't help her plan. Very few businessmen would want to join her in rejuvenating a bar in a backwater town, no matter how profitable she could make it. Not even Jake, and he loved the backwater town.

Not that she was thinking of Jake as a possibility for her plan. Jake, she knew, would never go back to business unless it involved spending all his mornings on a lake and left him a lot of free time to just stare at the sky. Jake had no ambition and wasn't going to have any. He was a nice man, but he was absolutely impossible.

But later when she dreamed, it was Jake who filled her fantasies, and by the time she woke up the next morning, she was feeling definitely uneasy about another morning on the lake. She was spending too much time with him. That's why she was dreaming about him. He was the only man she ever saw.

She called Rick and moved their hike up to nine, and then left a message with Will for Jake that said she wouldn't be going out with him that morning; she had a date.

Jake told himself that he wasn't annoyed that Kate had canceled. Three mornings on a lake did not make a tradition or a commitment or anything else. The reason he was annoyed, he told himself, was that she'd left the message with Will. Will had looked at him and said, ''You and Kate Svenson?'' and grinned, and Jake had said, "No," and stalked off. Of course not him and Kate Svenson. Extremely bad idea. Good thing she was only staying another week. Then she'd be out of his hair and things would get back to normal.

But maybe it wouldn't make any difference when she was going home. Maybe she'd be spending the rest of her time with Rick Roberts. Jake scowled across the lake into the woods where somewhere Kate was walking even now with Roberts. Jake had met him a few evenings before and liked him a lot; an easygoing, down-to-earth kind of guy, dedicated to his business because he was dedicated to saving the environment. He was, Jake had to admit, perfect for her plan. They could hug trees together and Kate would see that they made a fortune doing it.

Well, good, Jake thought. *That takes care of that annoyance. Sure is good to have the boat to myself for a change.* He slumped back down onto the cushions, slapped his hat over his face, and tried to go to sleep.

Rick was perfect for her plan, and Kate tried to feel happy about it. Rick had adjusted his stride to hers so she could keep up. He did not take her arm to help her over nonexistent obstacles, breathe heavily in her ear, or try to intimidate her with his knowledge, wit, or physical prowess. He was polite, funny, kind, interesting, and gallant. When she asked him about his business, he talked about the environment instead, telling her what could be done through consulting to ease the burden on the land, water, and air.

"I'm boring you," he said at one point, and Kate said, "No, you're not. I'm envious. I wish my work was that satisfying."

"We can always use help," Rick said. "Especially somebody with a mind as sharp as yours." He smiled down at her without guile. "If you ever want to join the firm, say the word."

He was the one, she told herself. This was it. She wasn't ever going to find anyone as great as him again.

So when he stopped at the edge of a trail deep in the woods and put his hands on her shoulders, lowering his mouth to hers, she kissed him back. It was a pretty good kiss.

When they broke apart, he smiled at her, stepped back to give her room, and promptly disappeared.

"Rick?"

He'd lost his footing and fallen over the side of the trail and rolled down a steep incline. Kate picked her way through the weeds and saplings down to where he'd landed, dazed, at the bottom.

"Are you all right?"

"Only my pride is wounded," he said, and she helped him up and kissed him again for being so sweet. It was still pretty good.

"I can face anything now," he said, smiling at her.

"Good." Kate was relieved. For a moment, it had looked like Jake's prophecy of disaster was coming true, but Rick was all right. He was going to make it through the whole date.

Kate started back up the hill. "I think we can get back up there if we use the saplings to pull us up."

Rick took one step and collapsed, his ankle turning under him.

"I'm sorry, Kate," he said, gasping. "I must have sprained it after all."

Don't panic, she told herself. *You are not cursed, Jake*

is an idiot, and Rick will be all right. "Lean on me. There's bound to be a trail down here that we can take."

As they moved off through the underbrush, she looked back to where he had fallen. The vines grew thickly there, and they all had three leaves. She thought of Jake. If he laughed, she would kill him in the boat and push his body into the lake.

They found a gradual incline, and Kate coaxed Rick up to a clearing in the trees. He was scratching every now and then.

Please let me get him back to the hotel before I do something else to him, she prayed silently.

When they reached the clearing, they found a deserted road, but it wasn't familiar and Kate had no idea which way to turn. Wonderful. Not only did Rick have a sprained ankle and terminal poison ivy, now she'd gotten him lost. He'd starve to death in the woods. They both would. But Jake would be wrong about one thing: If they starved together, this would be one man who had kept her until the end of the date.

"Sit here," she said. "I'm going for help."

He scratched his ankle. "I should come with you. It might not be safe."

"You're probably safer by yourself than with me anyway," she told him. "I'll be back."

Kate automatically turned toward the lake while she reviewed everything that had happened to her since she'd left the city. This was not working, and she really didn't know why. She'd had a perfectly good plan, and look at it now. The more she thought about it, the clearer it became that she and her plan were doomed. There were some forces in the universe that were too big for humans to comprehend. It was time to give up and go home.

She followed the shoreline until she saw Jake in his boat, floating under the willow.

"Hey," she called out to him and waved.

She saw him sit up, so startled that he rocked the boat. Then he saw her and put his head in his hands, and she knew he was laughing. She sat down on the shore and waited for him to row across to her.

When he got there, he pulled the boat up and walked over to her.

"Where's Rick?"

"Accident."

Jake started to laugh again. "You're like the Bermuda Triangle," he said, looking down at her. "They go out with you, but they don't come back."

"It's not funny."

He reached his hand down to her, and when she grasped it, he pulled her to her feet. "Is he still alive?"

"Yes."

"How bad?"

"Sprained ankle and poison ivy."

Jake shook his head and let go of her hand. "I'll go get the car."

They picked up Rick, Jake helping him carefully into the front seat, and drove him to the hotel.

"You're showing remarkable restraint," Kate said to Jake from the back seat as he drove. "Wouldn't you like to make a comment here?"

"I'm speechless. Maybe this is God's way of telling you not to date."

Kate sighed. "I've come to that conclusion, too. I didn't push him or anything, you know."

Rick turned to look at her over the seat. "What are you talking about?"

"I'm mad, bad, and dangerous to know," Kate said. "Me and Lord Byron."

"That's ridiculous," Rick said. "Let's have dinner tonight."

"Your insurance premiums will double," Jake said. "Kate's on the same list with asbestos and toxic waste."

"I insist," Rick said.

"Thank you." Kate smiled wanly at him. "But I have to work. I appreciate the offer, though." Besides, Rick was going to be hip-deep in calamine by dinner. She felt terrible. Just terrible.

Jake helped Rick up to his room, saw that his ankle was packed in ice, and then went back down to the lobby to collect Kate.

"Is he all right?" Kate asked. "I feel awful about this."

"About time you developed some guilt," Jake said, and then when he saw she was really upset, he said, "He's fine. Come on out on the lake and cheer up. I'll even let you have a beer. One. Don't guzzle it."

Even out on the lake, Kate couldn't shake her depression. It was time to quit. Have a good time with Nancy and Penny and Jake and then go home. Marriage wasn't everything.

"What's wrong with you?" Jake asked.

"I've decided to give up dating. It's too depressing."

"So the plan's off, huh?"

"Yes," Kate said, gloomily. "I'll probably never get married."

"I don't see why you wanted to get married anyway," Jake said. "You've got a career and friends and—"

"Oh, please," Kate said. "I don't need this. I get this from Jessie."

"Well, she sounds sensible. Listen to her."

"I don't understand why she doesn't understand," Kate said. "I know why you don't understand. You never get lonely and you don't need anybody else—"

"Hey…" Jake said.

"But I am lonely. That's why I kept saying yes to Derek and Paul and…and…"

"Terence," Jake supplied.

"I know he was Terence," Kate snapped. "I just wanted to make a life with someone. A life that wouldn't start at eight at night. I wanted to wake up with someone who had the same goals I did, and work with him all day, and then come home at night and be…"

Jake waited while she searched for the words.

"Be comfortable together, I guess." Kate let her head flop back on the cushion. "I've watched my father get married five times. I've watched his marriages end five times, including the time my mother walked out, and every time it was because he never saw any of them as partners. They were all something he'd acquired along the way, like the BMW and the condo. I didn't want that. I wanted to be a partner." She rolled her head sideways so she could see Jake. "Sorry. Didn't mean to bore you."

"That's okay," Jake said, cracking a beer and holding it out to her. "Drink this. You'll feel better."

"You drink it," Kate said. "I'm not thirsty."

"I don't care if you're thirsty or not," Jake said. "I'm trying to sedate you. Drink it."

Kate took the can. "Don't you ever think about get married?" she asked. "Don't you miss having someone around?"

"Married? No," Jake said. "Someone around? Maybe. Maybe somebody who's about eighteen, five foot two, and who thinks I'm God."

"The brunette at the hotel," Kate said gloomily.

Jake stopped with his beer halfway to his mouth. "What?"

"That little brunette," Kate said. "The one who's always hanging around you."

Jake looked puzzled.

"She was talking to you at the pool table the other night," Kate said patiently.

"Barbara Ann?" Jake looked confused. "She's just a kid."

"She's probably twenty, Grandpa," Kate said. "And you just said you wanted them short, young, and dumb."

"I didn't say dumb," Jake said.

"You implied it," Kate said. "I can't believe that's really the woman you want. You're just being obnoxious. What do you really want?"

"Well, I know better what I don't want. I don't want somebody who's always nagging me to be something I'm not. And I don't want somebody who thinks she knows what's best for me and who maneuvers around trying to get me to do things her way."

Kate frowned. "Nobody wants anyone like that. It's like saying, 'I don't want someone who'll poke me in the eye with a sharp stick.' Forget what you don't want. What *do* you want?"

"I don't know," Jake said. "Somebody fun. Comfortable. Somebody who does her own thing and leaves me alone." He looked over at Kate. "Pretty much the opposite of what you want, I guess. I don't want to build an empire with anybody. I just want to have a good time and come home to somebody warm at night."

"Jake, that should be easy," Kate said. "Any woman would do that for you. You can't have been looking too hard."

"I haven't been looking at all," Jake said, glaring at her. "I never even thought about it until you brought it up, thank you very much. Can we talk about something else?"

"Sure," Kate said and stared sadly up through the willow leaves.

"You tending bar at Nancy's tonight?" Jake asked, clearly desperate for a subject.

"Yes," Kate said. "Sally's not coming back for a week."

"You're doing a great job," Jake said. "A couple of people mentioned it last night."

"Thank you," Kate said.

"I'll beat you at pool again tonight."

"No, thanks," Kate said. "I'm going over the books with Nancy."

"Oh, right." Jake drank some of his beer. "So you've found a way to save the bar from the Yankees."

"Nancy's not worried about the Yankees," Kate said. "She'd just like to make a little more money, and I can show her some ways to make the bar pay better."

"You and Valerie," Jake said, and then spilled his beer when Kate surged up from her seat.

"I am *not* Valerie," she said through her teeth.

"Damn it, Kate! That was good beer," Jake said, sitting up and trying to blot the beer up with his shirt. "Of course you're not Valerie. Will you please snap out of it? So you're not getting married this week. You'll find some sucker in the city and be married before the year's over.''

''I don't want to marry some sucker,'' Kate said. ''Stop trying to get rid of me.''

''I'm not trying to get rid of you. Hell, I gave you beer.'' He glared at her again. ''Why are we fighting?''

''I don't know.'' Kate sank back down into her cushions. ''Maybe Penny had the right idea.''

''What right idea would that be?'' Jake asked, opening another beer.

''She's getting married and having twelve children and not working.''

''So she's up here looking, too? Maybe I should mention this to Will. Could be a whole new slant to our advertising.''

''No, she's already engaged,'' Kate said. ''He agrees absolutely that she shouldn't work. I can find men like that. Maybe I'm just asking too much.''

''I thought Penny was the little blonde who was dating everybody in the hotel,'' Jake said, confused.

''She is.''

''And she's engaged?''

''It's all right. She's just dating, and he knows about it.''

Jake frowned. ''And I thought only you got engaged to weirdos.''

''They weren't that bad,'' Kate said, staring up at the sky. ''I left Terence because he didn't want me to work.''

''What a fool he must have been,'' Jake said. ''You won't catch me stopping a woman from supporting me.''

''I can't believe Penny doesn't want to work.'' Kate

shaded her eyes and looked at Jake. "She wants to be a *housewife*."

"So?" Jake tilted his can and drank. "It's not prostitution. Leave her alone."

"Women fought for years so we could have careers," Kate said. "She's throwing it all away."

"I thought women fought for the right to choose to work," Jake said, putting his can back in the cooler. "I thought it was all about choice."

"You don't understand," Kate said.

"Sure, I do." Jake leaned back on the cushions. "In the bad old days, men kept women from choosing to work. In the bad new days, women keep women from choosing to stay home."

Kate opened her mouth and then shut it again.

"Come on," Jake said. "Tell me I'm a sexist pig."

"*I'm* a sexist pig," Kate said. "And a snob. And I'm not too bright."

"Oh, hell," Jake said, lying back down. "I like you a lot better when you're calling me names."

"I'm trying to do better," Kate said.

"Well, stop it." Jake pulled his hat over his eyes. "You were fine before."

Kate watched him try to fall asleep. He was right. Self-pity was boring. So she'd made a few mistakes. A lot of mistakes. She still had more than a week of vacation in front of her. She had Penny to laugh with, and Nancy to plan with, and Jake to drift on the lake with every morning.

She nudged him with her foot.

"What?" he said.

"Can I come out on the lake with you again tomorrow?"

He tipped his hat back. "Depends. Are you going to be over this poor-little-me fit by then?"

"I'm over it now. Thanks for the sympathy."

"You need sympathy like you need Derek and Terence and Paul. Are you playing pool with me tonight or not?"

"Yes," Kate said. "But I'm going to win."

"Oh?" Jake looked amused. "And what makes you think that?"

Kate batted her eyes at him once. "I'm not going to wear any underwear."

Jake looked at her for a moment and then pulled his hat back over his face. "Me neither," he said.

Wednesday night, things were always slow, Nancy told her. They used the time to clean and restock, talking and laughing together about disastrous dates past and future, and she gradually forgot to feel guilty about Rick. The bar was quiet with the low murmur of voices and the faint click of the balls from the pool table. As the time drew close to ten and all but the regulars had filtered out, Kate looked around and realized she knew everyone in the room by name.

She leaned on the bar and smiled at them all. Nancy, Jake, Will, Ben, Thelma, Henry, Early. Friends. Her eyes swept again to the back of the room where Jake was playing pool with Ben. He always looked taller and broader from the back. He was so easygoing and he always seemed to be just a minute away from laughing, and she'd look at his face and forget he was so big. But he was.

Then he bent over to make a shot, and his jeans stretched tight across his rear end. Nice rear end. She remembered how warm he'd been on top of her. If he were anybody but Jake...

"Don't lean over the counter like that. You're giving Rollie Beamis a heart attack," Nancy said.

"I love it." Kate turned around. "I know it's unliberated of me, but I love being a hot blonde in a low-cut top. I especially love it because I'm thirty-five. I figured sexual magnetism had passed me by, and now here it comes when I least expected it."

"I don't see why it's unliberated," Nancy said.

"I think the idea is to use your mind for power, not your body."

"Why? Men use their bodies to intimidate people every day."

"I don't think it's the same thing."

"Honey, use what the good Lord gave you, and since he did give you plenty, there's no reason why you shouldn't give others the pleasure of the scenery. Besides, the profits are up considerably since you started bending over the tables."

"Well, hell, let's shorten our skirts, then." Kate grinned at her.

"Is that part of this plan?" Nancy said, pulling Kate's notes out from under the bar.

"No," Kate said. "This plan is boring and practical. For instance, did you ever think about buying your liquor in bulk with Will up at the hotel?"

"No," Nancy said. "Why should I?"

"Major savings," Kate said. "Look..." She pulled her notes around and showed Nancy her figures.

"Where'd you get these numbers?" Nancy asked.

"From Will." Kate jerked her thumb toward the back of the bar where Will was sitting. "He's enthusiastic about the idea. And he said there's no problem with storing your overstock up there.''

"You talked about this with him?''

"Shouldn't I have?'' Kate looked uneasy. "He had the numbers. It's just a suggestion.''

"No,'' Nancy said. "No, it's great. I'm just not used to having somebody else doing things about my bar.''

"I didn't do anything,'' Kate said. "I just asked him.''

"Kate, it's all right. In fact, it's great.'' Nancy smiled at her. "In fact, it's more than great, it's wonderful. It's just that I've done everything by myself for so long, I was surprised.''

"Well, you're going to do this by yourself, too,'' Kate said, turning to the back of the bar. "Let me get Will, and you can work this out.''

"No, wait.'' Nancy caught her arm. "Show me the rest of the stuff you've cooked up first.''

They bent over the plans again.

Half an hour later, Nancy leaned on the bar and said, "This is amazing.''

"Well, if you like that, look at this,'' Kate said, and pulled out her master plan. "If you doubled the size of the bar, put in a stage and dance area, and added another twenty tables, you could handle the hotel overflow crowd. Your profits should—''

"Wait a minute,'' Nancy said, laughing. "Where would I get that kind of money? And how could I manage that big a place?''

Kate sighed. "I had a feeling you'd say that. I have this tendency to look at the bottom line and see profits first.'' She smiled. "I may have caught Will's employ-the-universe disease, too. This would create a few more jobs around here, give local bands some exposure, and bring more people down into town to see the shops. I just never stopped to think that it would also make life a lot more complex for you."

"Let me see that plan again," Nancy said.

Kate handed it over and shook her head. "You're right. You couldn't do it alone." She hesitated. "Do you suppose maybe Ben might help you manage the bar?"

"Only over my dead body," Nancy said absentmindedly while she studied Kate's notes. "One of the reasons we've been married for twenty years is that he has his life and I have mine. Twenty-four hours of togetherness would break us up in no time. And besides, I like running this place by myself. I don't need anybody else in here confusing me."

"Oh," Kate said. "Well, it was just a thought. I'll go get Will and you can talk over the liquor problem."

"You know, if I had the money for this..." Nancy began, but Kate was already gone.

At ten-thirty, Nancy called last drinks, and Kate dropped her tray on the bar.

"My feet are killing me," she said.

"Well, if you hadn't spent the morning hiking..." Nancy began.

"Is there anything that escapes this town?" Kate asked.

"Nope," Nancy said. "Who's on the schedule for tomorrow?"

"No one." Kate shook her head. "I've maimed enough hotel guests. I'm retiring. Besides, watching you and Ben has spoiled me. I'm holding out for love, and I don't think that comes with my plan." She leaned her back against the bar. "Although I've got to admit, I love being a local sex symbol. I can flirt with everybody and not get in trouble."

"Don't push your luck too far," Nancy said, grinning at her. "Men are only human."

"Oh, I'm careful who I flirt with." Kate smiled confidently. "I know who's safe."

Nancy shook her head.

"You floozies work here, or are you just holding up the bar?"

Kate turned and found Jake with his arms crossed, leaning on the bar behind her. "I don't mean to interrupt, but we've been signaling for beer for quite a while back there."

A lock of dark hair had fallen over his eyes, and his grin was warm and familiar, rakish under his mustache. He was so cute. Her buddy. She crossed her arms and leaned on the bar to mimic him, leaning over until her nose was an inch from his and their hats touched. "Maybe you just weren't sending the right signals, sugar," she drawled.

Jake looked at her, startled.

Then Kate saw his eyes darken and noticed the sudden heat that was there. She flushed and he smiled.

"I'll tell you what," he said, his voice low and husky. "You tell me the right signals, and I'll send them."

She went hot and then cold and then hot again, and his smile widened.

"Two beers, Nancy," he said without taking his eyes off Kate. "And hurry it up. I've been waiting a long time."

When he'd gone, Nancy said, "Do you want me to pour some ice water over your head?" When Kate didn't say anything, she added, "I warned you to be careful."

"What happened there?" Kate tried to breathe. "I feel like I just got hit by a truck."

"And about time, too. The past couple of days here, most people in the bar have been wishing the two of you would just sleep with each other and get it over with. The sexual tension is kind of getting to all of us."

"What sexual tension?" Kate asked. "We're friends."

"The sexual tension that just plastered you all over the bar," Nancy said.

Kate carefully didn't look back at Jake for fear her knees would go. God, she'd been stupid. "Am I the last to know?"

"Pretty much, although Jake ran you a close second. He's been so careful about women for so many years, and then you sneak up and poleax him from behind. I can't tell you how we've enjoyed it."

"We who?"

"Ben and I, for starters." Nancy leaned on the bar and laughed. "I'll never forget when he came in and told us all about you the first day he met you, laughing his butt off about you and a couple of guys at the luau. He said you were a cute kid. We had this picture of a sort of tomboy type, maybe twenty, not too together. Then here comes this cool blonde into the bar." Nancy laughed again at the memory. "Ben took one look at you that night and said, 'This boy is in trouble, and he doesn't even know it.' And sure enough, here we are. And of course, we've all thought for quite a while that it was about time Jake got serious about somebody, so we've just kept our fingers crossed. Everybody knew the two of you were going to end up together."

"How?" Kate asked dazedly. "Why?"

"It's a small town," Nancy said. "We've been watching each other fall in and out of love forever. Beats TV."

"I'm not in love with Jake." Kate took a deep breath. "And he's not in love with me."

"Hold that thought, honey." Nancy grinned at her. "It's not going to do you a bit of good, but it will steady you for a while."

Kate concentrated on not looking back at Jake. "I think I'm in trouble here."

"Why don't you go back in the storeroom and hunt me up another jar of olives," Nancy said kindly. "Take your time. Breathe deep. Put your head between your legs."

"Olives," Kate said. "Gotcha."

Nine

Jake went back to the table and began to play, but his eyes were full of Kate. She was the kind of woman who would get him into trouble. She was vulnerable and bright and funny and desirable—God, was she desirable—and he'd end up following her back to the city and before he knew it, the hat would be gone and he'd be shaving the mustache off.

Then he thought of Kate again, smiling at him. It might be worth it.

He tried to look at the pool table, but his eyes were still full of Kate. All his memories came back—Kate laughing at him in the boat, Kate in lace and satin after taking off her blouse, Kate stretched out across the pool table under him, Kate walking out of the lake.

He miscued, and the ball bounced off the table.

"That's going to cost you, buddy," Ben crowed and began to run the table.

Kate coming out of the lake. He closed his eyes and imagined her as she was then, imagined her under him as she'd been when they'd played pool; imagined her melting under him.

"Come on, ace. It's your turn."

Jake chalked his cue absentmindedly. Kate stretched out in the boat, her legs tangled with his. Kate stretched out on her bed, holding her arms up to him. Kate at the bar, her lips parted and her eyes half closed, telling him to send the right signals. Kate coming out of the lake.

He miscued again.

Ben stared at him. "Are you throwing this game?"

"What?" Jake asked from a long way away.

"Never mind," Ben said, and started his run.

Kate leaned against the shelves in the storeroom and tried to examine the situation logically. It was clearly impractical. Impossible. Jake was just a buddy. A good buddy. No, a great buddy. She remembered how much fun she'd had with Jake in the boat, how she'd felt with Jake's eyes on her as she walked out of the lake, Jake's leg carelessly touching hers in the boat, Jake's hand on her arm, on her back. Jake.... She breathed faster, thinking about him.

She heard a yell from outside in the bar. Somebody had just won a game of pool.

Jake was clearly impossible, clearly, intoxicatingly impossible.

She was in big trouble.

At that moment Jake came into the storeroom and closed the door behind him. He watched her as she turned to look at him, her eyes full of heat.

"Ben just beat me at pool." He stood in front of her with his hands on his hips.

"Good grief," Kate said. "What did you do? Fall on your cue?"

"I got distracted."

Jake leaned against the shelves, a hand on each side of her, and looked into her eyes. She suddenly had trouble swallowing.

"We seem to have been a little slow here, darlin'," he said, and bent down to kiss her softly. Time stopped, and Kate felt his lips distinctly on hers, not as a blurred impact, but as Jake's lips touching hers. *This is Jake,* she thought. *Jake. Oh, my God.*

His mustache tickled a little, and he tasted faintly of beer and something else that was hot and sweet and intrinsically Jake. She opened her mouth to taste him again, touching his lips with her tongue and leaning into his kiss, and he pulled her into him, bending her back under him as he kissed her harder. She felt the world spin around her and kissed him back mindlessly, pressing against him, clutching his shoulders until he broke the kiss and moved her head under his chin. She could feel the pulse at the base of his neck pounding, feel herself breathing fast against his chest.

"This isn't quite what I had planned," he said.

"I know," she said wildly. "Me either. Who cares? Kiss me again."

Jake cradled her face with his hands and kissed her softly once, twice, running his tongue over her lips, down her neck, kissing the hollow at the base of her throat. She trembled with wanting him, moving her hands over the muscles in his back, feeling them hard and tense under her touch.

"This is making me crazy," she said. "We have to stop."

"Right," he said, moving his hands away. "Right."

As he brought his hands down, he accidentally brushed against her breast and she moaned. He froze, and then moved his hands under her tank top, cupping her breasts, rubbing his thumbs hard across her nipples through the lace of her bra. She clenched her teeth and shuddered, pressing against his hands, gasping at his touch, running her tongue along his collarbone, his neck. He kissed her, his tongue thrusting in her mouth, his hands hard on her breasts, and she pressed her hips against his, crying out with need.

"Oh, God, Kate," he said.

She bit his arm through his shirt.

"We need to make love," he said into her hair. "For about two weeks. Right now."

She rubbed her face in his shirt. "Anything," she said breathlessly. "Just keep making me feel like this."

Nancy knocked on the door came in.

"Go away, Nancy," Jake said, holding Kate close.

"Kate's off now," she said. "Take the woman home."

"Good idea," Jake said. "I'll go bring the car around." He slowly let her go, touching her cheek once, and then went out the back door.

When he was gone, Nancy said, "You okay?" and Kate opened the large upright cooler and stuck her head in it.

"In the long run, I'm in terrible trouble," she said from inside the refrigerator. "In the short run, I'll be okay as soon as that man puts his hands on me again."

"Go for the short run," Nancy said.

Kate expected to be embarrassed when she got in the car with him, but all she really felt was heat. She was having a hard time breathing.

"I want you tonight," Jake said as she got in the car.

He took what little breath she had left away. The world looped around her.

"Good," she squeaked.

"We have to go to my cabin first for protection," he said.

Kate swallowed and tried to fight her way through all the images that swamped her. Jake's hands on her. All night. Jake touching her. All over. "Oh, God."

"Are you okay?"

"Just touch me," she said, and he put his hand on her leg, stroking her thigh while she breathed deeply beside him. She slid down a little in the seat, and his fingers moved higher, into the heat, until he slipped his little finger under the lace of her panties, and she slid down farther, to make it easier for him.

"Or we could just pull off to the side of the road here," Jake said huskily.

"Sounds good," Kate said, and he laughed softly and moved his hand away.

"We've been waiting a week," Jake said. "We can wait the ten minutes to my cabin."

"Yes, but I didn't know we'd been waiting a week," Kate said, leaning closer to him.

"I did," Jake said. "I just wasn't paying attention." He put his arm around her and pulled her close while he steered the car up the road to the cabin. "I'm paying attention now."

Jake parked the car at an angle in front of his cabin, and pulled Kate up the steps, kissing her as they went. He shut the door behind them and caught her to him, kissing her again until she clung to him, breathless. "We don't have to make up for the whole week tonight," he told himself out loud, and Kate said, "Yes, we do," and pulled him over to the bed, falling backward with him on top of her. They fumbled with each other's clothes, laughing at their own clumsiness until they were naked together. Then, suddenly, the laughter stopped.

Jake kissed her, holding her close to him as if savoring the feel of her against him, but Kate moved against him, urging him on. "Don't wait," she whispered, feeling him hard against her. "I want you now." Then he kissed her again, running his tongue over her lips and plunging it into her mouth, then moving down her throat to her breasts. He moved with an urgency she'd never seen in him, a savagery that fired her blood. When she cried out because he felt so good, he licked down her throat again to her breasts, nibbling there while she breathed in little gasps and moved under him. She pulled his hips against her, aching because he felt so hard against her, and she wanted him so much.

"Now," she said, and he said, "No," and smiled at her. Something inside her melted at that smile, and she relaxed and moved with him, giving herself up to his rhythm, making each second individual and alive because he was touching her. His hands caressed her, exploring her, and when she thought she couldn't bear it anymore, he moved his mouth down across the slope of her belly and into the blond curls between her legs, stroking there. And she arched her hips to meet his mouth and moaned, lacing her fingers through his hair and pulling his mouth against her, until she exploded inside, throbbing with white heat under his hands.

He moved his head up when she lay still again, and she felt his tongue hot across her stomach. He licked her breasts as he slid across her skin, finding her mouth with his just as she cried, "Oh, please, now," and then he suddenly moved hard into her, and she felt her blood surge again with the shock of him inside her. *Jake*, she thought, and lost her mind, writhing beneath him, clawing at him, pressing her hips frantically against him as he rocked inside her over and over until, finally, she came again, this time in great shuddering, clenching spasms, crying in her ecstasy and bringing him with her at the end.

They lay shuddering in each other's arms, until he could move, could reach down to pull the sheet over them, holding her close.

"I'm never going to get enough of you," Kate whispered, fighting for her breath. "Not if we make love forever."

He kissed her, murmuring her name as her lips touched his, and then they fell asleep, exhausted, in each other's arms.

When Kate awoke the next morning, Jake was still asleep. He was warm and solid next to her, and she put her cheek against his chest and thought of the night before; of how they'd laughed and slept and then made love again when Jake reached for her suddenly in the middle of the night, needing her so, touching off an equal need in her that they had both moved in frenzy to sate. They were perfect. She wanted him again.

He slept deeply beside her, exhausted to the point of oblivion. She eased herself out of bed, still feeling him throbbing in every cell of her body. He was so exhausted, she couldn't bear to wake him, but she needed his touch, needed to feel some relief on her body. She wrapped herself in his robe and walked down to the lake.

The sun wasn't up yet; there was only a faint pinkness in the sky. When she got to the edge of the lake, she dropped the robe and walked in, feeling the chill water bring her nerves to life. Jake made her feel this way.

Jake.

She plunged into the water, feeling the shock all over her body. Then she swam out to the middle of the lake, diving and twisting through its liquid coolness until all her heat and need were gone.

When she turned to go in, Jake was sitting where he'd been before, this time dressed only in his jeans. Just the sight of him made her breathless, hot again, and she forced herself to breathe deep before she swam to him.

She stopped when she was shoulder-deep in the water.

"Hello," she said.

"Morning," he said.

"Did you come to watch?"

He smiled, and she loved him so much she felt dizzy.

"Don't do that," she said. "I'll drown."

He shook his head. "I came to swim."

"Come on in." She gestured behind her. "Plenty of room."

"Are you naked?"

"Oh, yes. See?" She moved forward to him, walking slowly out of the lake. His eyes never left her body.

"I'll go in...when you come out," he said, and she laughed and moved toward him.

She walked up on the shore and stood beside him on the blanket. He was only inches away from her, just like before. But this time he leaned forward, resting his head on her stomach, sliding his hands up to her hips, and very gently licked his tongue into her.

The world reeled around her and she clutched at his shoulders. He looked up at her, standing shivering and wet in the pale dawn light. "That's what I wanted to do that morning," he said huskily, and pulled her down into his arms.

"You were the most beautiful woman I'd ever seen." He stroked his hand across her stomach. "I can't believe I've been so dumb about you." He dropped his head down to hers and kissed her, cradling her in his lap.

"I've been dumb, too," she said softly. "Me and my plan." She cuddled closer.

"You were never going to find anybody to fit that plan," Jake said, holding her.

"Well, actually, I did," Kate said. "Rick Roberts was perfect for it."

Jake frowned at her. "If he was perfect, what are you doing naked with me?"

Kate grinned. "He was perfect for the plan. You're perfect for me. Go figure." She pulled his head down to her and kissed him, and he sighed and held her close.

"I should go to work," he said. "But maybe I'll take the day off."

Kate rolled out of his arms and grabbed for the robe as she stood. "Go to work," she said. "I'll still be around when you get off."

When Kate got back to her cabin, Penny was sitting on the step, looking unhappy.

"Can I talk to you, Kate?" she asked.

"Of course." She sat down beside Penny. "What's wrong, honey?"

"I was with Mark last night."

"Well, that's nice. I think Mark is terrific."

"So do I," Penny said mournfully. "And I was with Mark *all* of last night."

"Well, good," Kate said, and then, as the full import

of what Penny was saying hit her, she added, "Oh. Not good."

"He's so sweet, and he makes me laugh," Penny said.

"Like a good friend," Kate suggested, thinking of Jake.

"And when he makes love to me, I lose my mind."

"Like a really good friend," Kate said, thinking of Jake.

"I think I'm in love with him."

"Well, that's great," Kate said, stealing a look at Penny. She didn't look happy. "Isn't it?"

"No," Penny said. "I'm getting married to Allan next month, remember."

"Well, yes, I remember. But, don't you think," Kate suggested cautiously, "that maybe, with this new development and all, you might be better off with Mark than with Allan?"

Penny shook her head. "Mark's in college. I'd have to wait years for a baby."

"Well, babies are great, of course," Kate said, "but I really think you'd be better off forgetting about the baby part and concentrating on the man part."

"I don't know." Penny looked confused. "I feel just awful about this. I've never cheated on Allan before."

"Well, maybe that's because you've never loved anyone before," Kate said, trying not to sound like the dating-advice column in *Seventeen.* "Why don't you spend some time with Mark and see how things work out. Maybe the feeling will wear off."

"Do you think so?" Penny asked.

"I hope so," Kate said, thinking of Jake. "We're in a real mess if it doesn't." She patted Penny on the leg.

"Come on. Let's have lunch and play tennis and forget about men for a while."

Kate played tennis with Penny for most of the afternoon because she wanted to move. She'd never felt so alive, so conscious of every part of her body. She and Penny swatted the ball back and forth without keeping score, laughing at each other and enjoying the afternoon sun and the sweat and their friendship. Several men stopped to stare, and Kate waited for Penny to drift over to them, but Penny stuck her tongue between her teeth and concentrated on returning the ball, oblivious to her admirers.

"I'm having so much fun," she told Kate when they stopped to towel off.

"Me, too," Kate said. "I think we're getting better."

"We couldn't get much worse," Penny said and laughed.

They went back to the court, and Kate grinned when she saw the men lined up at the chain-link fence to watch Penny serve. It never occurred to her that they were watching her, too.

At three, they walked to the bar in the hotel dining room for cold drinks, laughing and talking and swinging their rackets at nothing.

"This was a good day," Penny said as they went into the cool dimness.

"That it was," Kate said. She waved to Mark behind the bar. "Two colas. Non-diet. The hard stuff. Penny and I live on the edge."

Mark grinned at both of them as he poured the colas and Penny blushed. When he saw her turn pink, he blushed, too.

"We'll sit over here at a table," Kate said, trying to hide her grin. "We're too tired to balance on barstools."

Penny found a table in the corner and waited until Kate had joined her. "What am I going to do?"

"Do you have a choice?" Kate said. "Are you really going to be able to go back and marry Allan, feeling this way about Mark?"

"Maybe it's just a crush," Penny said.

"Maybe," Kate said. "But—"

"Hi, can I join you?" Valerie sank down in the chair next to them. "I'm just about at my wits' end."

"Oh?" Kate said, annoyed at the interruption. She looked over at Penny and saw that even she was frowning. It took someone with extremely bad social skills to annoy Penny. Valerie was hitting on all cylinders today.

"What's wrong?" Penny asked politely.

"What else? Men!" Valerie gave a short laugh. "Mark!" she called, without looking around. "Gin and tonic!"

Penny glared at her.

"Any man in particular?" Kate asked hastily, checking Penny for weapons. There didn't seem to be much she could do with a drinking glass unless she broke it on the edge of the table and used the jagged edge to go for Valerie's jugular. Kate pulled the glass out of Penny's reach just in case.

"Will!" Valerie said with real venom. "I can't believe he's so stupid."

"Will never struck me as stupid," Kate said.

"Well, he is. He refuses to talk about the new bar, and the longer we sit on that idea, the more money we're losing. And I've done everything but flat-out tell him that another hotel is trying to hire me away, and he just ignores me." She ended her tirade on a wail. "It's like he doesn't care."

"Maybe he doesn't," Penny said.

"Of course he does," Valerie snapped. "Damn it, I have a plan here!"

"Don't say that!" Kate said, wincing.

Mark brought Valerie her gin and tonic and winked at Penny before he went back to the bar.

"Yeah, plans are for the birds," Penny said morosely.

"What are you two talking about?" Valerie asked.

"Well, I have this friend, see?" Penny said, shooting a look at Kate that said "Shut up." "And she had a plan to marry a really steady wealthy guy so she could stay home and be a housewife and mother and have a lot of kids because that's what she really wanted. You know?"

"No," Valerie said. "But if that's what she wants, what the hell."

"And she found the perfect guy," Penny said gloomily. "And then she went and fell in love with a poor guy who's never going to have much money and won't be able to have kids with her for years."

"So what's the problem?" Valerie asked.

"What?" Kate said.

Valerie shrugged. "She stays with the rich guy. Love doesn't last. Money does if you know how to manage it." She looked at Penny. "Tell your friend to dump the poor guy, marry the rich guy, and take night courses in investing. That's what I'd do."

"I'm sure you would," Kate said. "Don't you love Will?"

"Well, of course I love Will," Valerie said.

"What if he didn't have the hotel?" Kate asked. "What if he ran the hardware store?"

Valerie thought about it. "Depends on the size of the hardware store, I guess. And what I could do with it."

Kate tilted her head and looked at Valerie appraisingly. "This isn't about money, is it?"

"What?" Valerie asked, confused.

"It's not the money, although you want that, too. It's the hotel and the wheeling and dealing and making plans. That's what hooks you."

"I guess," Valerie said. "What are you talking about?"

"Because that's what hooks me, too," Kate said. "I need the challenge. I can't just sit out on a lake and watch the fish for the rest of my life. I need to play the game." She bit her lip. "I hate it, but that's me."

"Why hate it?" Valerie looked at her like she was crazy. "You're terrific at what you do."

"Yes, but now it's getting in the way of what I want," Kate said.

"I can't believe you ever let anything get in the way of what you want," Valerie said. "I really admire that in you."

"Thank you, Valerie," Kate said, standing . "Excuse me a minute. I need another cola. This one with rum, I think."

That night at Nancy's was a madhouse, and Kate served drinks until she was dizzy. Three days ago, she'd been a customer. Tonight she was a pro.

She took a beer and a wine cooler to Brad and his date, and he grinned at her and said, "Thanks, Kate."

Three days ago he'd been groping her. Now it was "Thanks, Kate." He'd better leave a big tip.

She poured colas with rum and without. She plopped

olives into martinis and dipped tequila glasses in salt. She filled the pretzel bowls on the bar over and over again. She carried drinks all over the bar, neatly dodging hands that came up to pat her rear end, telling drunks their next drink was coffee, taking several orders at once and delivering them without a mistake.

I'm pretty good at this, she thought. It was a nice thought, and as she was feeling particularly happy anyway, and as she happened to be passing Jake as he bent over the pool table, she patted him on the rear end to celebrate.

He miscued.

"God, I hope you stay forever," Ben told her, and she laughed and went on to serve drink after drink after drink.

Jake watched her as she threaded her way through the crowd, smiling at everyone, leaving a trail of grins behind her. She looked like she belonged there. She did belong there. With him.

Then, like an evil curse, the thought intruded: *What would she do here? There's nothing for her here. And you remember what happened the last time you fell for a smart blonde with a great body? It didn't last. What makes you think you're any smarter this time?*

"Are you going to play pool?" Ben asked.

"Yeah," Jake said shortly, and shoved his thoughts about the future away. He'd think about that later. Much later. After all, he wasn't even sure how he felt about her.

He looked up to see Kate walking past Brad, who reached out a hand and caught her on the rear end before she had time to swerve. She spilled some beer on him, and he laughed.

Jake put down his cue.

"Back in a minute," he told Ben and walked over to Brad.

He put one hand on the back of Brad's chair and the other on the table in front of him and leaned over.

Brad looked up.

"Hey, Jake," he said happily.

"Don't touch Kate," Jake said.

Brad looked up, and his smile faded.

"If you get my drift," Jake added gently.

"Got it." Brad nodded. "Sorry about that."

"No problem." Jake patted him on the back and ambled back to the pool table. Ben rested on his cue and grinned at him.

"It was a lot easier when we could just brand 'em," Ben said. "Then everybody'd know not to mess with our womenfolk."

"Shut up and play pool." Jake picked up his cue.

"I never thought I'd see you lay claim to a woman," Ben needled him. "Right in front of the whole bar and everything."

"I just don't think she should have to put up with that." Jake glared at him, annoyed. "Are you going to play pool or not?"

"I'm going to play pool." Ben chalked his cue. "Funny it never bothered you when Thelma and Sally had to put up with that."

"Thelma and Sally can take care of themselves."

"And Kate can't?" Ben laughed. "Kate could take care of all of us. If we put her in uniform, we wouldn't need the marines."

"Nancy can take care of herself, too. What would you do if Brad went after her?"

"The same thing that you did, buddy," Ben said. "Which is my point, exactly."

Jake stood still for a second and then thought, *Yeah, right. I'm not sure how I feel about her. Oh, hell.*

He moved around the table. "Hit the ball," he said to Ben. "Try to actually get one in a pocket this time."

Above all, Kate served beer. Long-necked bottles, mugs, glasses. She felt like Mickey Mouse in "The Sorcerer's Apprentice." After a while, she leaned against the bar and saw beer bottles marching toward her, sloshing foam over her feet. The world was made of liquid.

"Kate!"

She shook herself awake and turned to Nancy.

"Take a break," Nancy said. "It's ten. We're slowing down."

"How can you tell?" Kate asked. The bar was still packed with people, the noise was still as loud.

"Because we're talking to each other instead of slinging drinks. You want to go sit down for a while?"

"No." Kate looked back at the table she'd just served. "Watch the guy in the blue T-shirt. I think he's had enough."

"Right." Nancy nodded. "I'm going to hate it when you go. You're getting almost as good at this as I am."

When she went. She kept trying to avoid that thought and it kept hitting her in the face.

"Hey, Nancy, two more over here," Early called.

Nancy turned to make the drinks and saw the expression on Kate's face. "You are going, aren't you?"

"Yes," Kate said numbly.

"Just checking. I thought you might have changed your mind, with Jake and everything." Nancy shoved the tray over the bar. "These go over to Early and Ross at the far pool table."

"I see them." Kate picked up the tray and then stopped. "I can't give up my whole life after one night," she said to Nancy. "That would be stupid. He's never said he loved me, and how could he? We've only known each other a week. Less than a week."

"I know," Nancy said. "But I don't want you to stay just for Jake. I want you to stay for me." She leaned on the bar. "I've got a lot of friends here, people I grew up with, but you and I...talk. About the bar and other things. I'm going to miss you."

"I'm going to miss you, too," Kate said with tears in her voice. "I'd better get these to Early."

"I didn't mean to upset you, honey." Nancy patted her hand. "We've got more than a week before you leave. Let's just enjoy that. Here, take a couple of beers to Ben and Jake, too. They're due."

Kate took the tray back to the corner of the bar, handing Ross his whiskey and Early his gin. "Thank you, Kate," Ross said. "Mighty kind of you, Kate," Early said.

"My pleasure, boys," she said and smiled because it really was. There was something about being in a place where you knew everybody and everybody knew you. Like home.

She took the beers to Jake and Ben.

"Pat his butt again," Ben told her as he watched Jake sink a ball. "I almost won a game when you did that."

"If you only almost won, what good will it do?" Kate asked.

"Well, do something else, then," Ben grumbled.

"Hell, we're paying you minimum wage. Earn your keep."

Kate put down the tray as Jake came around the table to take his next shot. "Come here, big boy." She hooked her fingers in the waistband of his jeans and pulled him toward her. Then she kissed him full on the mouth and heard someone whoop behind her.

She'd expected him to pull away, but he leaned into her, bending her back onto the pool table as he slipped his tongue in her mouth. Her hat fell off. He took his time about finishing the kiss so she broke it off, and when she pulled her mouth away, he kept her pinned to the table and said, "Did I ever tell you my fantasy about pool tables?"

"No!" She slipped out from under him, red-faced.

He clapped her hat back on her head.

"Don't start what you can't finish," he said, grinning at her, and turned back to the table.

Ben was shaking his head at him.

"We were going to put up a big sign that said Jake Templeton Finally Got Laid, but now we won't have to."

"What's this 'finally' stuff?" Jake looked insulted. "I wasn't desperate." He studied the table and found his shot. Then he lined up his cue and remembered Kate bent under him in the same position. If he hadn't had a fantasy about pool tables before, he had one now.

He miscued.

"One more great athlete destroyed by sex," Ben said and began to run the table.

"Very nice," Nancy said when Kate got back to the bar.

"I don't know what got into me." Kate pulled her hat low over her eyes.

"On a guess, Jake."

"Very funny."

"You sure you're going to leave?" Nancy asked. "It seems like you were always here."

"I'm sure," Kate said. "I need to work and there's nothing for me to do here. And besides, I don't think Jake's interested in anything permanent. The whole idea of me staying is just impossible."

There was a loud cheer from the back of the bar. "Kate, I love you," Ben called out to her.

"That's twice Ben's won in a week," Nancy said. "If that can happen, anything can happen."

The four of them closed the bar at midnight and walked out to the parking lot behind the bar.

"I can't believe I beat you," Ben said, savoring his victory. "Twice in one week."

"I was distracted." Jake put his arm around Kate to pull her close. "You'd better give her a raise."

"Women," Ben said. "You gotta love 'em." He moved behind Nancy and put his arms around her.

She closed her eyes and leaned back against him, smiling. "Twenty years. And you still turn me on like crazy."

"If we're in your way, just say so," Jake said. "Otherwise we'll stay and watch."

"Good idea," Ben said. "Maybe you'll learn something."

"Not if you make love like you play pool."

"Hey, I *won*."

"Come on." Kate tugged on Jake's arm. "I'm tired, and I'm covered with beer, and Nancy's getting all the action."

She pulled him toward the car.

''Your problem is you're not aggressive enough,'' Jake told her. ''A man likes a woman who will show a little interest. You keep playing hard to get and you never will get—''

''Get in the car,'' Kate said. ''I'll show you aggressive.''

The next morning, Kate came home to find Penny weeping hysterically on the steps.

Kate took her into the cabin and washed her face with cold water.

''What's wrong?''

''I made my decision.'' Penny swallowed and sat down on the bed. ''I decided the only smart thing to do was to stay with Allan, so I told Mark I was getting married. He got so mad....'' Penny shook her head.

''Well, he has a point.'' Kate sat down beside her. ''How would you feel if the situation was reversed, and you'd been sleeping with him, and then he told you he was engaged?''

''I thought guys didn't care. I thought they just liked the sex, you know?''

''I don't think Mark is a 'guy.' I think he's a person. I think he really cares about you.'' Kate took a deep breath. ''I know you really care about him.''

Penny began to cry again. ''What am I going to do?''

''Call Allan and tell him it's all a mistake.''

''I can't. The wedding's all planned. We have caterers. My dress is done.''

''You're going to spend the rest of your life with a man you don't love because of some caterers and a dress? Are you out of your mind?''

''Yes,'' Penny said and cried some more.

"What do you want me to do, Penny?"

"Fix it." Penny looked at her like a little girl.

"I can't, kid," Kate said. "You've got to fix this yourself. Choose one or the other."

"Allan."

"Okay. Then it doesn't matter that Mark is mad. Because you're never going to see him again anyway."

Penny howled and threw herself on the bed.

"Come on, Penny." Kate patted her on the back. Funny. She'd never thought of herself as a patter.

"You don't understand," Penny sobbed. "You have Jake forever."

"No, I don't." Kate swallowed hard as she remembered. "I'm leaving in a week."

A week. Seven days.

Penny lifted her head from the bed.

"Why?"

"Because I have a career in the city and—"

"You're leaving Jake for a job, and you tell me *I'm* out of my mind?"

"It's different," Kate said weakly, moving to sit on the edge of the bed.

"Does Jake know?"

"Yes." *He must know. We haven't talked about it, but he must know.*

"I bet he doesn't." Penny wiped her tears on the back of her hand. "He's crazy about you."

"Not that crazy," Kate said grimly.

Penny sat up beside her. "We didn't do so hot, did we?"

"No, we didn't," Kate agreed. "But we're not done yet. I think you'd better do some fast thinking about Mark and Allan."

Penny gulped.

"Imagine living with Allan for the rest of your life," Kate said. "Imagine never seeing Mark again."

"You think I should stay with Mark," Penny sniffed.

"I think you don't have any choice," Kate said. "If you're this unhappy when he's mad at you, how are you going to feel if you never see him again?"

Penny threw herself back onto the bed and began to cry again, and Kate sighed and handed her more tissues. *And how am I going to feel?* she asked herself as she patted Penny. *I feel like throwing myself down beside her and howling, too. This is a mess, but I'm not going to think about it now. I'm going to enjoy myself, damn it. I'll think about the future later.*

Much later.

Ten

The rest of Kate's vacation passed in a pleasant, lazy blur of floating on the lake with Jake in the mornings, playing with Penny in the afternoons, bartending in the evenings, and then making love with Jake with such passion that she forgot there was anything in the world but the two of them. Periodically, the cold threat of the future sliced its way into her consciousness, but she repressed it ruthlessly. She wasn't leaving until Saturday. She'd think about it later. Not now.

The week was hardly without its distractions. She worked on the plans for the bar with Nancy and felt a satisfaction she hadn't felt for a long time as things began to fall into place there. Knowing Nancy's possessiveness about the bar, she was careful not to overstep at first, but Nancy seemed genuinely enthused about the changes she proposed, and finally Kate relaxed and enjoyed working with her.

At the hotel, she watched Donald Prescott pursue Valerie with the single-minded passion of a businessman pursuing a profit. Valerie did everything but throw him in Will's face, and Will remained oblivious throughout. So Valerie grew more determined.

And, of course, Jessie called.

"Are you engaged yet?" Kate heard her say as she picked up the phone.

"What happened to 'Hello'?"

"Hello. Are you engaged yet?"

"No, and I'm not going to be," Kate said. "I'm in love with a man who's allergic to marriage."

"Jake's allergic to marriage after one bad assistant district attorney? He sounded tougher than that."

"How did you know I was talking about Jake?"

"Oh, please," Jessie said. "It was so obvious. Once I heard you'd been drinking beer with him in a rowboat, I knew it was just a matter of time. So, does he fill all the important requirements of your plan?"

"Important requirements?"

"You know," Jessie said. "Great sense of humor. Equal rights for women. Terrific in bed. Loves you to the point of madness?"

Kate thought about it, surprised. "Yes," she said slowly. "He does. What do you know, he does."

"Good," Jessie said. "You may marry him."

"I don't think so," Kate said. "I don't think Jake is ever getting married again."

"Ha," Jessie said.

"You don't know Jake," Kate said.

"No, but I know you," Jessie said. "You'll find a way. Now what do you want on your wedding cake?"

"Fish," Kate said, Jessie's certainty cheering her up. "And a rowboat."

"You got it," Jessie said. "I'll start designing it now.'

And on Thursday, after an intense game of tennis and an even more intense conversation back at the cabin, Kate held Penny's hand while she made a tearful call to Allan and broke off their engagement.

"I did the right thing, didn't I?" she asked after she'd hung up and Kate was blotting her tears.

"Why don't you go discuss it with Mark?" Kate suggested. "See how you feel?"

"Do you think he'll even talk to me again?" Penny said.

"It's a sure thing," Kate said. "Begin by mentioning you're no longer engaged because you're in love with him and will be until the end of time."

"All right," Penny said. "But even if he doesn't, I'm glad I broke the engagement. Allan was really nasty on the phone. I wouldn't marry him now, even if Mark doesn't want me."

"Well, that's good to know," Kate said. "Come on. I'll walk you down. I need to tell Jake I'm running late anyway."

Jake and Will were conferring at the lobby desk when they walked in, so Kate stood by the door to the bar and watched Penny try to talk to Mark. He looked at her warily when she walked in, and then she leaned across the bar and said something. He dropped the glass he was holding, vaulted the bar, and pulled her into his arms.

Kate grinned and turned away, thinking, *I love a happy ending. I wonder if Jake can jump over a bar like that.*

She was heading toward the desk to ask him when Valerie caught up with her.

"I've been looking all over for you," she exclaimed and put her arm around Kate.

"I have to talk to Jake and go," Kate said quickly. "I can't possibly play pool tag or anything else."

Valerie laughed. "Don't be silly. I want to talk to you about us."

"Us?" Kate said, confused. "What 'us'?"

"You and me," Valerie said. "We're going to be spending a lot of time together and, frankly, I couldn't be happier. Now that Jake's settling down—"

"What?" Kate asked, trying to disentangle herself. "I don't know—"

"Now don't be coy," Valerie said. "Everybody knows about you and Jake."

"Oh, great," Kate said.

"It'll be just the four of us," Valerie began. "I know it's too soon for you and Jake to set a date—"

"Uh, Valerie—"

"But Will and I will be making an announcement *very* shortly," Valerie said, looking *very* pleased. "I don't know why I was so upset before. I should know by now that that's just the way Will is."

Kate shot a glance at Will behind the lobby desk. "Valerie, have you actually discussed this with Will?"

"Well, in a manner of speaking, of course," Valerie said.

"Not 'in a manner of speaking,'" Kate said. "In a manner of sitting down and you saying, 'I think we should get married,' and him saying, 'Yes.'"

Valerie shook her head. "That's not the way Will and Jake are," she explained. "They don't like confrontation. You try that and you'll never get anywhere." She lowered her voice. "They're both very stubborn."

"I know," Kate said. "But I don't think…"

Valerie patted her on the arm. "Trust me. I know the Templetons." She smiled at Kate. "After all, I'm going to be one. And if you play your cards right, so will you."

Kate looked at her, appalled. Valerie hadn't even talked to Will. She just assumed that she knew what was going on.

Kate looked up and saw Jake crossing the lobby toward her. Of course, she hadn't talked to Jake, either. And she was running out of time. *I'm no better than Valerie,* she thought. *I've got to stop hedging around. Jake would want me to be up-front about this.*

"Jake's not like that," she told Valerie.

"You'll see," Valerie said. "They're all like that."

"I've got the order forms for Nancy," Jake said, coming up behind her. "You want to run them down now or wait until this evening?"

"This evening," Kate said. She took a deep breath. "We need to talk."

"Why?" Jake asked suspiciously.

Valerie waggled her finger at Kate. "I warned you," she said and left them to join Will at the desk.

"Tell me you're not planning something with Valerie," Jake said.

"I'm not planning something with Valerie," Kate said. "What are we doing here?"

"We're standing in the lobby," Jake said. "Is this some game?"

Kate stood her ground. "No. You and me. This thing we're doing. What is it?"

"This thing?"

"This relationship," Kate said.

Jake groaned and stepped back. "I hate that word."

Kate looked over at the desk. Valerie was standing close beside Will, shaking her head at Kate and smiling. Jake's retreat was obvious from clear across the lobby. "Fine," Kate said, and turned away.

Jake caught her arm and turned her back. "Look, this is not the time or place to talk about it."

"Fine," Kate said. "Where and when?"

"Later," Jake said, looking around the lobby. "Much later. Someplace else."

"I'm going home day after tomorrow," Kate said.

Jake jerked his head back to face her. "Saturday?"

Kate nodded. "My reservation is up Saturday morning. I have to be out of my cabin by noon."

Jake looked relieved. "Well, hell, if that's the problem, move in with me. You practically have already, anyway."

"Jake," Kate said. "I have a job. A career. I can't play house with you forever."

"Is that what you want?" Jake asked. "Forever?"

Kate stopped for a minute, took a deep breath, and then said, "Yes."

"Oh," Jake said.

"Thank you," Kate said, turning away again. "This clears things up nicely."

"No, it doesn't." Jake grabbed her arm again. "Damn it, stop walking away from me and give me a chance to think."

"Haven't you thought about this at all?" Kate asked him, her anger finally breaking through. "Hasn't it once occurred to you in this past week that this was going to end?"

"Yes, it's occurred to me," Jake said. "I've just tried not to dwell on it."

"You know what one of the most annoying things about this is?" Kate asked him through her teeth.

"What?" he said uneasily.

"Valerie was right." Kate wheeled around and walked away before he could stop her.

"Hey," he said and followed her to the lobby desk.

"Sorry, Valerie," Kate said. "Next time I'll listen."

She turned to leave and Jake blocked her path. "Wait a minute," he said, and she said, "No," and opened the first door at hand, and went in, slamming it in his face.

"That's my office," Will said to Jake. "Not that I mind, but I may need it later. Anything going on here that I should know about?"

"No," Jake said. "I will handle this." He opened the office door and went in, closing it behind him.

Kate was standing in front of the desk, visibly trying to keep calm. She wasn't doing a very good job of it.

"Okay, I've been a jerk," Jake said. "Let's talk."

"Let's not," Kate said. "I'm so mad at you, I could kill you. Go away until I calm down."

"Running away would be a cowardly thing to do," Jake said. "I'm not a coward."

"Running away would be the wise thing to do," Kate said, warning him.

"Well, I'm not wise, either," Jake said, moving toward her.

Kate backed away until she bumped into the desk. Then she exploded. "You make it very clear that you hate women who manipulate around an issue instead of confronting it. Then when I try to confront it, you try to evade the subject."

"I know," Jake said. "I told you I was a jerk. You just sort of sprung it on me, and I dropped the ball." He held out his arms to her. "Come here. I'll make it up to you."

Kate ducked out of his way. "How?"

"Well, I thought we'd neck," Jake said, grinning.

"You can't be serious," Kate said, edging toward the door.

"I'm always serious," Jake said and grabbed her. She kicked out at him and he dodged her, tripping over the edge of the carpet and dragging her to the floor with him when he fell.

"Ouch!" Kate said and tried to roll away, but he pinned her under him.

"Listen to me," he said. "You're right. We have to talk. I'm sorry."

"Not sorry enough," Kate said, trying to push him off her.

His arms tightened around her. "I'll be as sorry as you want. Just tell me how." He tried to concentrate on what she wanted, but she was soft and warm, wriggling under him in his arms, and all he could think about was how good she felt. Almost automatically, his hand moved up and cupped her breast.

Kate glared up at him. "You're apologizing *and* groping me, at the same time?"

"It was just a reflex." He grinned down at her.

She looked indignant, but there was warmth behind the glare. *I know her,* he thought. *I know when she's angry and when she's just trying it on. And right now, she's just trying it on.*

She moved to roll away from him. "Some apology."

He rolled with her, and she landed on her back again, still under him. "You're not mad."

"Bet me," she said and swung at him. He caught her fists with his hands and pulled her arms over her head, pinning her to the floor.

"This is going to look great if Will walks in," she said conversationally.

"He's not that dumb." Jake ran his tongue down the opening of her blouse, which gave him another idea. "How much time have we got before you go to work?"

"Not enough. Get off me. I need a shower."

"I thought you tasted pretty salty." He let her arms go but stayed on top of her, kissing her neck.

"Get off. You weigh a ton."

"You've never complained before." He bit her earlobe.

"I was turned on before."

"Well, I'm working on that," he said and moved his hand to her zipper.

"No!" She shoved at him hard and pushed herself out from under him, standing before he could reach her again and backing away from his hands. "I've got to go to work."

"Feeling better?" he asked lazily, propping his head on one hand.

"Yes." She straightened her blouse. "Now that you're off me, and I can breathe, I'm feeling much better."

"You have a real mean streak, woman," Jake said, getting up. "Good thing you have a nice body."

"Very funny," Kate said and walked toward the door.

Jake caught at her arm and stopped her, suddenly serious. "Look, I'll pick you up at the cabin later and take you to Nancy's," he said. "And then, as much as I hate this, we'll talk tonight when you get off work. You were right. We've got to talk about this."

Kate bit her lip. "Thank you," she said. "I'm sorry I blew up like that. I've just been putting off dealing with this for so long, and then when I finally got the courage up to face it, you didn't want to." She leaned against him. "I'm truly sorry."

"Good," Jake said, patting her back. "We're both sorry. Equal guilt. You sure you don't want to neck?"

Kate pushed him away and laughed. "Later." She opened the door and crossed the lobby, and when she reached the outside door, she looked back and saw that he was leaning in the office doorway, watching her walk away. She put a little more sway in her hips as she left the hotel.

That's mine, Jake thought. *That swing is for me.*

An incoming guest turned to stare at her and stumbled on the step. *Don't bother, buddy,* Jake thought. *The lady goes home with me tonight.*

The bar was crowded for a weeknight, but by nine, things had calmed down to the point that Nancy, Will, Jake, and Kate could spread the finalized notes out on a corner table and talk.

"This makes so much sense I don't know why we didn't think of it sooner," Will said. "And it's not just the liquor. Look at the glassware." He shook his head. "It's brilliant." He looked at Kate. "You're brilliant."

"Thank you," Kate said. "But it's not that great. This is what I do for a living." She shrugged. "This is pretty much business as usual for me." She pointed to a notation on the plans. "Now this part is fascinating. Look at the shipping totals for..."

Jake watched her face as she explained her notes to Will and Nancy. She was so beautiful, but she was so much more. What the hell would she do, stuck in Toby's Corners? And what the hell would he do, stuck back in the city? No wonder he'd been avoiding talking about this. He was going to lose her.

Kate looked up and caught him looking at her and smiled. "Hey," she said. "Aren't you proud of me?"

"Very," he said without smiling back, and she looked concerned.

"Are you okay?"

"I'm fine," he said, and when she still looked worried, he held out his hand to distract her. "Let me see your figures. You probably screwed them up. Women are no good at math."

Kate shoved the plan across to him. "Do you feel all right?"

"Yes," he said and bent to look at her notes. "Aha," he said. "You forgot to add the depreciation on the glassware."

"You can't depreciate glassware, you moron," Kate said and reached for her plan back.

"Listen to the expert, kid," Jake said and the two of them began to argue while Nancy and Will listened, growing more and more surprised.

"I can't believe it," Will said to his brother finally. "She's got you talking business again. It's a miracle."

Kate winced, and Nancy kicked Will hard under the table, but the damage was done. Jake dropped the plan on the table and glared at Kate.

"Don't look at me like that," she said. "You're the one who asked to see the plan, and you're the one making dumb statements about depreciated glassware."

Jake opened his mouth to retort, but before he could get the words out, Valerie showed up with Donald in tow and put a chill on the conversation.

"Where have you been?" Valerie said to Will. "I've been looking all over for you."

Will clenched his jaw for a moment and then visibly forced himself to relax as he turned away from her. "Here," he said evenly. "Nancy and I had some things to talk about."

"What things?" Valerie said suspiciously.

"We're going to order everything for the bars together from now on," Will said, keeping his back to her, unaware of the storm in her eyes. "It'll save us both a bundle. Kate came up with the idea." Will smiled over at Kate. "She is one smart cookie."

"Is she?" Valerie said. "We need to talk about this."

Nancy and Kate glanced at each other, but Will seemed deliberately oblivious to what was going on.

"Why should we talk about it?" Will said. "It's a great idea, and we're going to do it."

"But what about *our* bar?" Valerie said evenly.

"What about it?" Will said. "It's doing fine."

"Not the dinner bar," Valerie said. "Our *country* bar."

"We don't have a country bar," Will said. "We don't need one. We have Nancy's."

Valerie put an arm around Will's shoulders as she stood beside him, and they all saw him stiffen. "But darling, I thought we agreed—"

"No, you didn't." Will glared at her. "I told you when you came up with that idea that we weren't going to do it."

"Well, I think it's a fine idea," Donald said. "I think you should listen to Ms. Borden. I certainly would if she were in my employ."

"Who the hell are you?" Will asked, peering at him in the dim light. "Oh. Prescott. What do you want?"

"Well, actually, I want your social director," he said, laughing nervously. "I know I told you I was a stock-broker, but actually—"

"I know," Will said tiredly. "You're a scout from Eastern."

"You knew?" Valerie said, dropping her arm from Will's shoulders.

"Well, then, we can put our cards on the table," Donald said. "I've just offered Ms. Borden a very generous contract, but she insists on giving you the opportunity to match it."

Will looked at Valerie for a moment and then turned back to the table.

"She's yours," he said.

"Ouch," Kate said, and even Jake winced a little.

"What?" Valerie said. She moved her hand to Will's shoulder and pulled him back in his chair to face her.

"Go with my blessing," Will said, patting her hand once and then prying it off his shoulder.

"What about us?" Valerie said, clenching her teeth.

"What 'us'?" Will said. "Hey, don't think I'd stand in your way on something like this. I wish you all the luck in the world. Eastern is the big time. Go for it." He turned back to Nancy and said, "So, do you agree with this ordering idea?"

"Absolutely," Nancy said, keeping a wary eye on Valerie. "Do we need to sign anything?"

"Naw," Will said. "We operate on trust around here."

"Trust?" Valerie said, her voice rising to a shriek.

"Trust? Three lousy years, and all I get is 'Good luck,' and you call that trust?"

Will turned back to her. "Oh, come on, Valerie," he began, and then she picked up his beer mug and threw the contents of it in his face.

"I thought so," Nancy said and slipped out of her chair to get a towel.

"Hey," Jake said, getting up, but Kate caught his arm and pulled him back down.

"Will's a big boy, and he got himself into this," she told him. "He can get himself out."

"Don't bother with two weeks' notice," Will was saying quietly to Valerie while he dripped on the floor. "Just leave me an address so I can forward your mail."

"Just like that," Valerie said.

"Val, it was always just like that," Will said. He took the towel Nancy handed him and blotted the beer off his face. "I thought you knew that. You never asked for anything else."

"What do you mean, 'He got himself into this'?" Jake said to Kate.

"They lived together for three years," Kate said. "Obviously there were expectations there."

"Three years," Valerie said with venom. "I thought—"

"No, you didn't," Will said. "I never told you I loved you, and you never told me. The one thing we had going for us was honesty. Don't blow that now. Go off with Prescott and have the career you've always wanted. This place was too small for you, anyway. You've always hated it."

"You won't forget me," Valerie said.

"That's for sure," Will said, and turned back to the table.

Valerie turned and walked away, with Donald Prescott trailing in her wake.

"Sorry about that," Will said. "Now where were we?"

"What do you mean, 'expectations'?" Jake asked Kate.

"Do you want to fight about this?" Kate said.

"Oh, hell," Will said. "Don't. It's over. Why should you fight about it? Personally, I'm relieved."

"I know you are," Kate snapped. "It's the worst thing I know about you."

"Hey," Jake said. "He didn't ask for any of this."

"Yes, he did," Nancy said. "I've got no time for Valerie, but she got screwed on this."

"Feel free to discuss my personal life," Will said.

"You owed her more than 'She's yours' after three years," Kate said.

"He did not," Jake said. "Stay out of this."

"She's hurt," Kate said. She looked over at Will. "It wasn't kind."

"I don't believe this," Jake said angrily.

"Being kind to Valerie," Will explained, "is a waste of time. She only hears what she wants to hear unless you're so blunt that you're rude."

"Maybe," Kate said. "But that was brutal."

Will looked over at Nancy and she nodded.

"Okay," Will sighed and stood. "I'll apologize."

"Are you out of your mind?" Jake said.

"I didn't say I'd take her back," Will said. "It won't hurt me to say I was a jerk. Maybe I was. We were together for three years. Maybe she deserves a better goodbye.''

"No, she doesn't,'' Jake said. "She's a bitch. She tried to run Nancy out of business and you into marriage. She deserves exactly what she got.''

"Nobody deserves what she got,'' Kate said.

Jake glared at her, and she glared back.

"Well, at the least the two of you are communicating,'' Will said with a slow grin. "That's more than Val and I ever did.''

"Communication like this, I don't need,'' Jake said, and pushed his chair back.

"Where are you going?'' Kate asked.

"Away from you,'' Jake said and stalked off toward the bar. Will shook his head and followed him, saying something to him and slapping him on the back before he went out the door to find Valerie.

"What's wrong with Jake?'' Nancy asked. "He never gets mad, and now he's been tense all night.''

"We've had a bad day,'' Kate said. "I'm leaving day after tomorrow, and we have a few things to work out. Such as whether we're ever going to see each other again.''

"Day after tomorrow?'' Nancy sat back in her chair. "So soon?''

"Well, I have this career,'' Kate said. "It's not much, but it keeps me in French Provincial furniture and Kentucky vacations.''

Nancy looked unhappy. "When are you coming back?''

Kate sighed. "From the looks of Jake at the moment, never.''

"He's not that dumb," Nancy said. "He'll get over it."

Kate looked over at Jake, hunched over the bar, his whole body still tense with anger. "Not any time soon," she said. "Not unless I do something about it."

"Well, do something about it," Nancy said. "He may be a big enough fool to throw what you've got away, but you're not." When Kate didn't answer, she stole a glance at her. "Are you?"

Kate stared at Jake's back. "No," she said. "I surely am not."

At ten, Jake took Kate home in silence.

"Come down to the lake with me," she said.

"I'm tired."

"No, you're not." Kate could feel her temper rise. "You're mad at me because of what Valerie did. That's dumb. Come down to the lake with me."

"No." He kissed her on the cheek. "Good night."

"Fine." She got out of the car and slammed the door. "But I'm going. And when you find my poor drowned body in the morning, you'll have no one but yourself to blame."

She started down the path, and after a few moments she heard him behind her.

Damn right, she thought. *I'll teach you to sulk, buddy.*

Kate kicked off her shoes and threw her hat on the shore, and then she pushed the boat into the water and climbed in. Jake caught the prow just as she picked up the oars.

"Where are you going?"

"The willow. I want to see it at night."

He climbed in. "Give me the oars, or we'll be out here all night."

When they got there, Jake rested on the oars without tying the boat up. "How long do you need to look at the willow?"

"Not long." She stood up in the boat and took off her vest.

"Oh, hell. Not now, Kate," Jake said. "Sit down. You're going to tip us over."

"The thing is," Kate said, ignoring him, "if I were a man I'd be straightforward about this and just say, 'Jake, you're being a real jerk about this because I am not and never have been either Valerie or Tiffany, and you have no right or reason to assume I ever will be.'"

She stripped off her tank top, and the motion made the boat rock a little.

"Very funny," Jake said. "Sit down, damn it." He reached up to pull her down and she stepped back, making the boat rock even more.

"Furthermore, you know as well as I do that Valerie had a point back there in the bar. You just don't want to admit it. If I were a man, I'd point out that that makes you a duplicitous jerk."

"Hey," Jake said.

"But I'm not a man," Kate continued. "I'm a woman. So instead of confronting you with the truth, I will manipulate you into a better mood by taking off my clothes and seducing you."

She unzipped her skirt, pulled it up over her torso, and threw it in the bottom of the boat.

"Kate, it's not going to work. I'm not in the mood."

Then she stretched in the moonlight, dressed only in her black lace bra and bikini panties, and he gave up.

"That's dangerous," he said.

"Stretching in a boat?"

"That, too," he said, and she knew she had him.

Kate grinned at him. "I knew you'd come around. We women always get our men by manipulation." She unhooked the front clasp of her bra and started to pull it open, but then she stopped. "No," she said virtuously. "This is wrong. It's wrong to manipulate men, even if they are behaving like morons." She hooked her bra again.

"Kate," Jake began.

"No, I'm going to handle this the right way," she said, her hands on her hips, looking down at him sternly. "The manly way. I'm just going to tell you frankly and honestly that you're a jerk and make you row me back to shore."

"Right," Jake said, and grabbed her arm, jerking her down on top of him. The boat rocked wildly, and she shrieked and held on to him.

He ran his hands up her back. "You didn't really want to go back to shore, did you?" he asked.

"Of course not," Kate said. "I'm not the moron in this boat." She relaxed as the boat stopped rocking and began to bite him on the earlobe.

"I've been wondering how you were going to kill me," he said conversationally as she straddled him and unbuttoned his shirt. "The other guys got pushed over cliffs and kicked by horses. Me, you're going to kill with sex."

She moved down to unzip his jeans and pull them off, and he ran his hands along her sides as she balanced above him.

"Where do you get all this fancy underwear?" He ran

his fingertips across the lace. "Do you belong to some kind of club?"

She bent to kiss his chest, and he unhooked her bra, pulling it down over her arms and then running his fingers lightly over her skin, cupping her breasts.

Kate eased away from him, her tongue moving slowly down across his stomach, feeling his muscles there tense under her lips.

"Kate?"

She dug her fingernails into his sides and moved her mouth between his legs, stroking her tongue across him and nibbling on his thighs. "Kate!" He laced his fingers in her hair as she took him in her mouth. She heard him gasp and felt his fingers tighten in her hair, and then she thought only of him, moving against her tongue, growing hard in her mouth. She forgot the moonlight and the lake and everything but Jake.

A few minutes later, she felt his hands reaching down to drag her, gasping, across his body.

"Oh, God, Kate," he said, drawing a ragged breath.

"You still complaining?" she whispered.

"Me? No." He pulled her pants down over her thighs and stroked her until she moaned. She pulled away from him and kicked her pants off, and then eased herself down onto him, straddling his body in the moonlight, crying out a little as he thrust up to meet her. She swayed, and he braced her hips with his hands to keep her erect so he could watch her, and she moved over him until the rocking of the boat against the water blended with the rocking of her against him.

"You're silver in the moonlight." He ran his hands across her skin. "I'm going to remember you forever like this. You're burned in my brain."

She looked down at him, and she swelled with so much heat and love for him that she was dizzy. *I'm going to love him until I die,* she thought. *Who have I been kidding? The hell with a plan. This is all there is.*

"Come down here." His hands were hard on her as he urged her down. "Come down to me before you lose control and hurt yourself."

She shook her head. "I'm not ready yet."

"Want to bet?" He shifted his hips, rolling against her, over and over until she gasped as the first wave of her orgasm hit her. He arched up to catch her as she fell against him, holding her tightly to him as the spasms took her, pulsing up into her to keep her moaning his name, until she was finally quiet in his arms.

Then, holding her hips against his, he rolled over and moved into her as if he were part of her, finding the rhythm of her blood, and she felt herself drowning again, felt the tension build and her muscles clench as he moved with deliberate slowness inside her. The pressure made her blood pound, and she moved to ease the need, only to burn with more. He slammed his hips against hers, moving faster and faster, plunging into her until she thought she'd break. "Don't stop," she cried, but he was beyond her voice now, and when she writhed under him as she came, he whispered her name and thrust hard into her one last time. From far away she heard a sharp crack, and then he moved against her again and shuddered in her arms, and she wrapped her arms tighter around him and held him as he fought for his breath.

"I've never had anything like this, Jake," she whispered. "Not like this that I have with you."

He kissed her slowly. "You're a miracle." His lips

moved over her, tasting her. "You're going to kill me, but you're a miracle just the same."

She laughed weakly, exhausted to the marrow of her bones.

"You're such a wimp," she said from beneath him, her voice muffled in his shoulder. He felt so good on top of her that she didn't want to ever move.

"Tell my mother I thought of her at the end," Jake said into her hair.

"You thought of your mother just now?"

"I meant at the end of my life. Don't tell her we were doing this."

"You're not dying, you big baby." She rolled her head back and realized that they weren't under the willow anymore. Jake hadn't tied the boat up, and they'd drifted to the middle of the lake.

"This is pretty," she said. "Look at the moon."

Gradually she realized there was something wrong.

"Jake, have you noticed the wet spot is bigger than usual?"

"Hmm."

"Jake, I'm all wet."

"I don't care," he said into her neck. "I'm not making love to you again tonight. I have to be able to walk around tomorrow."

"Not that kind of wet." She pushed him off her and sat up. "The boat is leaking."

"What?" He put his hand between the cushions where her hip had been. The boat was filling with water. "I knew I heard something crack a while back. I thought it was my spine. Thank God, it's just the boat."

"Just the boat?" Kate grabbed her tank top and pulled it on over her head.

"I was wrong." He lay back against the cushions, exhausted and happy. "You're not going to kill me with sex. You're going to drown me."

"Jake, the boat is going down."

"So did you." He smiled at her in the moonlight. "Have I mentioned that was great?"

She grabbed the front of his shirt and shook him. "Jake!"

He sat up slowly. "What do you want me to do? Sing 'Nearer, My God, to Thee'?"

"You, fool," she said and started to laugh. "Where's my underwear? It cost a fortune."

There was a good two inches of water in the boat now and it was sinking faster. Jake fished around and handed her underpants and bra to her.

"Here. I don't know where your skirt is."

"I can't swim in it anyway." Kate grabbed for her vest. "I don't believe this."

He reached for his pants. "It was a good old boat. I'm going to miss it."

"You're going to go down with it if we don't get out of here." Kate rolled over the side of the boat and into the water.

"I found your skirt," he said.

"Jake!"

"Will you relax?" He rolled over the side to join her, holding a bundle of his pants and her skirt. He still had his cowboy hat on, she noticed.

I'm in love with a lunatic, she thought. *Boy, am I in love.*

By the time they swam to shore, the boat was gone.

She wondered if that was symbolic of their relationship, and shivered. The timing was definitely right. Because great sex notwithstanding, she could feel a sense of impending doom. It hadn't been pretty in the bar tonight. And they still hadn't talked about the future.

Maybe because they didn't have one.

She looked over at Jake, who was staring out at the lake where his boat had died. She didn't want to talk about it tonight. She knew it was cowardly of her, but she wanted one more warm night with him before they faced reality.

He glanced over and saw her staring at him. "Are you all right?"

"I'm fine," she said and put on her underpants.

"You killed my boat," Jake said, putting on his. His jeans were wet so he threw them over his shoulder with her skirt.

"I'm not the one who pounded on the boards until they broke," Kate said. "In fact, I feel a deep kinship with that boat. I know just how it feels."

"Well, it died in a good cause." Jake put his arm around her. "Let's go back to the cabin before somebody catches us out here in our underwear."

Mark and Penny were sitting on the cabin steps when they got back.

"You're probably wondering about the underwear," Jake said.

"Not me," Mark said, looking at Kate's legs as she went past him into the cabin.

"I am," Penny said, and Mark put his hand over her mouth.

"No, she isn't," he said.

"You get a raise, kid," Jake said, and followed Kate

inside. "Mark and Penny?" he asked her when the door was closed and they'd stripped off their wet clothing.

"Yes, isn't it nice?" Kate pulled him down with her and snuggled next to him. "She dumped her fiancé for him and they're getting married. They're so happy. And Penny says he's great in bed."

Jake moved away from her a little. "Yeah, but can he sink a boat?"

"Oh, go to sleep," she said and pulled him close to her with a little more force than necessary. He kissed her forehead and held her tightly until she finally fell into a restless sleep.

When Jake woke up the next morning, she was gone. He pulled on his jeans and went down to the lake and found her sitting on the stony shore, staring out across the green water.

"You know this lake fetish you have is beginning to worry me. Should I put an aquarium in the bedroom?"

Kate turned her head and looked at him. "I guess I'm going back to the city."

Jake looked at her for a long moment. "I know," he said. He sat down gingerly beside her on the stones and stared out at the lake.

"And I don't suppose you're coming," Kate said, trying to keep her tone light.

"No."

Kate swallowed. "I'll stay here. If that's what you want."

"And do what?" Jake turned his head to face her. "Even if every business in Toby's Corners hired you as a management consultant, you'd be done in a week. Two, at most." He shook his head. "I thought about this last night while I watched you with Nancy and Will. You were amazing. And you were so happy.'' He smiled ruefully at her. ''I hate it, but there's nothing for you here.''

''Well, there's you,'' Kate said, and Jake laughed.

''Yeah. There's me.'' He turned away. ''It's not enough.''

''You might let me decide what's enough for me,'' Kate said tartly.

''Okay.'' Jake faced her again. ''Is it enough? Think of all those long days here with nothing to do.''

''Well, I'm thinking about the long nights with you, too,'' Kate said.

''Yeah.'' Jake turned away and squinted up at the sun. ''But the physical stuff doesn't last.'' He picked up a stone and skated it across the water.

''I beg your pardon?'' Kate glared at him. ''We are more than just 'physical stuff.'''

''We don't know that,'' Jake said. ''After a week? We don't know that.''

''So all you think of me as is a great lay,'' Kate said.

''Well, of course not,'' Jake said, and then he added, ''But I do think it's too soon to start giving up careers—''

''Or taking up one,'' Kate snapped, suddenly overwhelmed with frustration and anger.

''What?''

''You've been retired for five years now. Isn't it about time you got back in the game?''

''I don't want back in the game,'' Jake said. ''I want to stay here and—''

''Float on the lake? It's too late. Your boat sank.'' Kate felt all her repressed anger tighten in her chest. *Be calm,* she told herself. *There's no reason to get upset.*

This is a civilized conversation between two civilized people.

"I keep thinking," she said, "of what Will said last night. To Valerie."

"I don't want to talk about that," Jake said crossly. "I don't want to fight about that again."

"She said, 'Just like that,' and he said, 'It was always like that.'" Kate looked at him. "That's us, isn't it?"

"No," Jake said. "I love you." He swallowed. "I think." He tried again. "I just don't…" He paused, searching for the right words.

"I know," Kate said, gritting her teeth. "I know everything you don't. You don't want to go back to work. You don't want to be hassled. You don't want to get married. Everything with you is a negative. Every sentence about the future starts with 'I don't.'"

"Look," Jake said, annoyed. "I never pretended to be anything different."

"That's pretty much what Will said last night. Now tell me the one thing we've got going for us is honesty."

"What do you want, Kate?" Jake asked tiredly.

"I want a career and a husband. No," she said as he started to speak. "I want a career and you as my husband. No substitutions."

"Well, you can't have it," Jake said. "I'm not going back to any city, and I'm not going back to work. And you're not going to find enough work here to keep you happy." He looked over at her for a moment and then he smiled without humor. "They lied to you, kid. You can't have it all."

"At least I'm trying to get it," she said. "I'm not rolling over and playing dead."

"Kate," Jake began, but she overrode him.

"You know, all that drivel about you wanting the simple life out here, that's garbage. You don't want the simple life, because you don't want *anything*. You don't want anything because you're *afraid* to want anything. All you know is the safe stuff, the stuff you don't want."

"Hey," Jake said. "You're not exactly doing all that great with your own life, sweetie."

"At least I'm trying," Kate shot back. "At least I'm still in the game. No wonder you defended Will last night. He was doing a gold-medal performance in your favorite sport—running away." She stood and dusted off the seat of her pants while she glared down at him. "I'm so mad at you, I could kill you. And at the same time, I love you so much, I can't stand it." She shook her head at him, so angry that she could hardly speak. "You could come to work in the city if you wanted to. You could in a minute. And you'd love it. You know you would. You did once. You did last night. I saw you working on those plans. I saw how interested you were. Everybody saw it. We *could* have it all, damn it. You make me so mad...." Kate gritted her teeth to keep the scream that was rising in the back of her throat.

"Why don't we wait until you've calmed down..." Jake began reasonably, and Kate did scream.

"What the hell?" Jake surged to his feet and reached for her, and she stepped back, glaring at him with red-eyed intensity.

"Don't you ever patronize me," she snapped. "Don't you ever imply that we're arguing because I'm out of control."

"Well, hell, you're acting like a banshee," Jake said. "What am I supposed to do?"

"You're supposed to answer me," Kate yelled.

"You're supposed to tell me how you feel, get mad at me, do anything but sit there looking like some good ol' boy Buddha with all the answers."

"Buddha?" Jake said. "I know you think I'm godlike, but Buddha?"

"It won't work." Kate took another step back. "I'm not going to play any more word games with you. That's part of our problem. We were so good at being cute together, we never bothered to be real." Kate shook her head. "I love playing around with you, Jake, but I want real life, too."

"Kate, does everything have to be a damned soap opera? Can't we just be us together?" Jake gestured helplessly.

"No," Kate said. "We don't even know what 'us' is. You don't even know who you are. Or what you want to be when you grow up." She glared at him as her anger started to well up again. "And it's time to decide, Jake, because you're up."

"You know—" Jake said, glaring back at her, so mad he had to start his sentence over again. "You know who you're starting to remind me of?"

"Let me guess," Kate snapped back. "Tiffany. Valerie. Every woman you've ever known who didn't roll over and say, 'Gee, Jake, it's wonderful that you're wasting an incredible mind and a great education by staring into the lake.' Every woman who ever looked at you and made it obvious that she thought you were turning into a vegetable. You know why you hate all of us so much, Jake?"

"Because you're pushy, scheming, manipulative, power-mad bitches?"

"No," Kate said evenly. "Because you know we're

right." She turned on her heel and strode back to the cabin.

"The hell I do," Jake yelled after her when he'd recovered from his surprise, but she was already gone.

Jake took most of his anger out on some brush he'd been putting off clearing from the south end of the resort. The digging and hacking wore out his body, but his mind went plodding on, reliving the morning in glorious Technicolor. Kate was wrong, he knew. Absolutely wrong. But he hated fighting with her; hated not knowing if, when he saw her again, she'd smile at him like always, just because he was there. Finally he gave up and walked to her cabin, but when he got there, he saw Kate closing the trunk of her car. She was dressed in the same silk suit he'd first seen her in, her hair neatly rolled in a chignon.

"Kate?"

She started, and then turned around and smiled at him, a little too brightly. "I'm going to go ahead and take off now." She shrugged a little. "There's really no reason to stay, and I can beat the Sunday traffic."

Jake felt his chest tighten and took a step forward. "Kate, listen, I..."

"No." Kate bit her lip and then said, "I was... I didn't really have any... It wasn't my place... Those things I said this afternoon...." She frowned, trying to find the right words. "I'm sorry. You have a right to do what you want with your life, and you were obviously perfectly happy before I showed up and will be again as soon as I'm gone, so..." She smiled and shrugged. "I'm going."

"Oh," Jake said. "So, this is what you want?"

"No," Kate said. "But this is what I've got." She

took a deep breath. "Maybe you're right. It's too soon and too fast and maybe this is just physical and..." She stopped and swallowed again. "And it really hurts too much to stay here anymore," she finished. "It's going to be easier on both of us if I just go."

Jake stood there helplessly, trying to think of the right thing to say, but there wasn't any right thing. And finally, Kate kissed him on the cheek. Then she got into the car and drove away while he stood in the road and watched.

It's better this way, he thought, and wasn't convinced. "It's better this way," he said aloud, firmly, and turned back toward his own cabin.

He still wasn't convinced.

Eleven

A month later, Jake sat in an Adirondack chair on the back veranda of the resort with his feet propped on the rail, watching the sun rise over the lake, and tried to feel content. It wasn't happening. The old nagging feeling that he used to get had grown into a full-fledged monkey on his back, and it had been making him miserable and irritable since Kate had driven away. People had taken to avoiding him whenever necessary, and even Ben had lost patience with him finally.

"Look, if you're that unhappy, do something about it," he'd said the night before, slapping his cue down on the table. "Just stop taking it out on the rest of us."

Jake had slapped his own cue down and stormed out of the bar, feeling equally angry and stupid.

The feeling had stayed with him all night and into the morning and was plaguing him still. *Come on, Jake,* he told himself. *You live in God's country, you are gloriously free, you have no responsibilities and no real worries. You've got it made.*

Somehow it wasn't enough. "I've got it made," he said aloud, trying to convince himself. Will, who was backing out the door to join him, carrying two steaming coffee mugs, snorted with contempt.

"You're disgusting," Will said, looking down at him.

"What did I do now?" Jake asked.

"Well, you've alienated everybody in town, for starters," Will said. "I can't believe you were mean to Mrs. Dickerson."

"I wasn't mean to Mrs. Dickerson," Jake said, taking one of the cups. "I just said that cowboy hats looked stupid on women."

"She was wearing a cowboy hat."

"She was?" Jake frowned. "Damn. I didn't notice."

"It was bright red." Will hesitated and then plunged on. "This is about Kate, right?"

Jake glared at him.

"Well, it's obvious when she drives away, and you start acting like Godzilla immediately afterward." Will glared back at him. "Call her."

"It's not Kate," Jake said and got up to move to the rail and stare out at the lake.

"Yeah, right," Will said.

"No," Jake said. "I miss her like crazy, but it's not Kate. I mean, she's part of it, but it's more." He shook his head. "Something was wrong before she got here. She just made it worse."

"So, what is it?" Will sat down to listen.

Jake went over all the possibilities before he forced himself to face the awful truth. "I'm bored," he admitted.

"Hallelujah," Will said. "The dead walk."

Jake turned and sat on the rail to face his brother. "I'm not leaving Toby's Corners. I like it here. I belong here."

"So I was wrong," Will said. "The dead are only staggering, but it's a start. We'll take it."

Jake sipped his coffee and thought for a moment.

"Have we got any money?" he asked, oblivious to Will's sarcasm.

"Sure. We're rich."

"No." Jake looked at him patiently. "Money. The real stuff. Not the hotel, not the land. Money."

Will considered. "I've got a fund stashed away for emergencies. It's not much. Maybe fifteen thousand."

"I want it," Jake said.

Will started to make a smart comment and stopped. "All right," he said. "Will I ever see this money again?"

"Well, I don't know," Jake said, grinning down at him. "You should have thought of that before you started calling me a potted plant and introducing me to pushy blondes."

"Speaking of pushy blondes," Will began, and Jake shook his head.

"I don't want to talk about her," he said.

"I'm sure you don't," Will said. "Question is, what are you going to do about her?"

"I don't know," Jake said, looking back out over the lake. "I'm considering my options."

"That ought to keep you occupied for the next twenty years," Will said with disgust. "You're real good at considering your options."

Jake scowled down at him. "You're starting to sound like Kate."

"Well, she's an intelligent woman," Will said. "We've got a lot in common." He cocked a skeptical eye at his brother. "I don't care about the money or whatever it is you're going to do with it. But if you think playing around with it is going to make you a happy man, think again. This is about Kate and you know it.''

"I keep thinking," Jake said, "that if I could just get her back down here, we could work everything out." He frowned as he thought. "She was happy here, she just didn't have anything to do. But she was happy here." He looked back at Will. "Wasn't she?"

"Yes. She was. Get her back," Will said.

"How?" Jake asked him.

"Well, you could try calling her and asking her to come back," Will said.

"No," Jake said. "There's nothing down here for her. I can't ask her to come down here just for me."

"You're pathetic," Will said.

"Not pathetic enough to expect her to give up her life just because I want her back," Jake said. "There's got to be another reason for her to come back. There's got to be another way to get her back."

Will looked at him with disgust. "Have her kidnapped. Tell her you're pregnant and she's the mother. Leave a trail of bread crumbs."

Jake scowled at him. "I don't think Kate likes bread crumbs. I need help here. You are not helping."

"Well, then, leave a trail of something she likes," Will said, getting up to leave. "Just do something instead of moping around looking like a kicked dog and snarling at everybody." He left, banging the screen door behind him.

"The only thing she likes is managing other people's businesses," Jake said to nobody in particular. And then after a moment, he added, "And me." It was a new approach, and it brought to mind a new option. He sipped his coffee and stared at the lake while he considered it.

Then he put his mug down on the rail and went to Nancy's.

Two weeks later, Kate sat in her luxurious office, speaking patiently into her phone with Chester Vandenburg, the vice president of a company that she had been working night and day for the past six weeks to save. Part of her furious concentration was because the company had six hundred employees and four times that many stockholders, and she felt an edge of panic every time she focused on how close the whole thing was to going under. All those people. All those poor people.

The other part of her concentration was an effort to avoid remembering how much she hated the city, how much she despised her job, and above all, how much she missed Jake.

"All right, Mr. Vandenburg," she said, trying to keep her voice even. "Would you like to explain to me why you just voted the CEO of your failing company a million-dollar raise?"

She tapped her pen hard against the desk as she listened to his dulcet tones explaining the need to cherish good management. "Good management is the backbone of industry, Miss Svenson, and surely—"

"That good management is shipping your firm right down the tubes, Mr. Vandenburg," Kate interrupted, still tapping her pen savagely. "It's *Titanic* time over at your place, and you just gave the iceberg a mil for ripping a hole in your hull. Have you any idea of the view your stockholders are going to take of this? Roughly the same view that the passengers did on that other disaster, except that this time, Mr. Vandenburg, this time it will not be women and children first. This time everybody's going

down with the ship. Do you feel any guilt about this at
all, Mr. Vandenburg? About the employees and stockholders you just screwed? Have you any moral fiber
whatsoever?''

She stopped when she heard her voice rising to a
shriek.

His voice came over the line, oily and unctuous. ''I
don't think you understand big business, Ms. Svenson.
Perhaps if—''

''I was raised on big business, Mr. Vandenburg. I cut
my teeth on stocks and bonds and wrote my first school
paper on leveraged buyouts. My third-grade teacher was
quite impressed. I cannot help but feel, however, that she
would be even more impressed with the magnitude of
your ability to ignore what is happening under your nose
at the same time you are facilitating it.''

''Are you accusing me of impropriety?''

''Either impropriety or ineptitude on a truly magnifi-
cent scale,'' Kate snapped. ''With you, possibly both.''

Mr. Vandenburg cleared his throat ominously. ''Perhaps it would be better if the firm of Bertram Svenson,
Ltd. assigned someone else to our little problem,'' he
threatened.

''What a good idea,'' Kate said. ''I suggest the SEC.''

She heard a click on the other end of the phone as Mr.
Vandenburg hung up, and then her door opened.

''It's just me,'' Jessie said as she backed in holding
two waxy white paper bags. She dropped them on Kate's
desk. ''Sugar and caffeine,'' she said. ''Apple fritters and
black coffee. You look like hell.''

''Thank you,'' Kate said. ''I feel like hell. I always
knew I worked with scum, but I never realized it was
this bad.'' She pulled a foam cup from the bag and pried

the lid off. "This smells good. Are the fritters from Debbie's?"

"Yep. She sends her love and said to tell you that business is great and she's thankful for your advice every day."

"I need more Debbies and fewer Vandenburgs," Kate said. "Unfortunately, it's a Vandenburg kind of town." She sipped her coffee and stared wistfully at the fritter Jessie shoved in front of her.

"Who's Vandenburg?" Jessie asked as she opened her own coffee.

"One of several jerks I am currently trying to keep from financially murdering their own companies." She sighed and then looked at her best friend, who was blithely chomping away on a fritter. "You know, I used to enjoy this, but now... I'm losing my edge, Jess."

"You?" Jessie snorted. "Never. How many morons did you slash today?"

"Not enough," Kate said. "I want to stay and fight the good fight, but this is ridiculous." She leaned back in her chair. "I'm so tired of this, Jessie."

Jessie dropped her fritter on the floor in surprise. "You're kidding. That's *great*."

She bent to pick up her fritter and Kate said, "No, it isn't. This is my career."

"You have a very clean floor," Jessie said, examining her fritter. "There's no dirt on here at all." She bit into the doughnut again, chewed, swallowed, and said, "So have this career somewhere else. Like, say, Kentucky."

"No," Kate said.

"You'd go back if Jake wasn't there," Jessie said. "You miss it."

"Maybe," Kate said. She pulled her fritter toward her

and looked at it sadly. "I'm so miserable, I'm not even hungry."

"You miss Jake, too," Jessie said. "I can't believe you're being such a wimp about this."

"I am not a wimp," Kate said. "It's been six weeks, and he hasn't called. He probably wouldn't recognize my name."

"Oh, please," Jessie said. "Spare me."

"He's probably forgotten I exist. Six weeks." She looked at Jessie, the hurt plain in her eyes. "Six weeks, and he hasn't even called once. I've given up checking my machine. I buried it under my dry cleaning because every time I go home there's either no blinking light or, worse, there is one and it's somebody trying to sell me something." She shook her head and gestured to her office. "This is all I've got, Jess. And I hate it."

Her secretary buzzed her again. "Tim Davis of Davis Enterprises on two."

"Yet another jerk," Kate said and picked up the phone. "Hello, Tim."

"What the hell is this about not laying off the Princeton plant?"

"It's not cost-effective," Kate said. "The money you save in the layoffs will be counteracted by your retraining fees and start-up costs when the plant kicks into gear again. Also, it's very bad PR, laying off people who have worked for you for twenty years." Kate clenched her jaw to keep from screaming. "That kind of thing is right up there with ripping off the pension fund. And speaking of the pension fund, I was just going over some interesting figures."

"Who the hell are you working for?"

"My daddy," Kate said. "He's a son of a bitch, but

he never stole from widows and orphans. Clean this up, Tim."

He hung up on her, and she dropped the phone back in its cradle. She looked over at Jessie and said, "I hate this. I hate this, I hate this, *I hate this*."

"What you need here," Jessie said, "is a plan." She reached across Kate's desk and pulled a memo pad toward her.

"Oh, no, I don't," Kate said.

"Why not?" Jessie said. "It worked before. Give me a pen."

"Yes," Kate said. "It worked beautifully. That's why I'm back here, lonely and miserable...."

"Now as I recall," Jessie said, ignoring her, "first we set goals. In this case, I think the goal should be to get you married to Jake." She stretched her arm across the desk and took Kate's pen.

"Jessie," Kate began, and Jessie overrode her again.

"Now, what's keeping you from marrying Jake?"

"Well, he's not speaking to me, and that's a real drawback," Kate said, sarcastically.

"We don't know that he's not *speaking* to you," Jessie said. "We just know that he's not *calling* you. There's a difference."

"At the moment, it escapes me," Kate said, but Jessie wrote down, *"1. He won't call,"* and then looked at Kate again. "What else?"

"Jessie," Kate said, but Jessie said, "Look, the man loves you. You love him. And I'm going to get you back together. What else?"

"He *thinks* he might love me," Kate corrected. "He was still pondering the question when I left."

"Okay," Jessie said and wrote, *"2. He thinks he might*

love her.'' She looked down at the list and said, "This is coming along nicely. What else?"

"Well," Kate said, seething as she thought about it, "he hates confrontation. But he also hates women who manipulate him, which pretty much cuts off all form of human contact except sex."

"How does he feel about sex?"

"He's heavily in favor of it," Kate said, wondering gloomily if he still was, and if so, with whom.

"Okay," Jessie said, and wrote down, *"3. He hates confrontation and manipulation."*

"Plus," Kate said, "he's not working. He's just wasting himself, and that drives me crazy."

"Well, it is his life," Jessie began, and Kate overrode her.

"It's a terrible waste and he knows it. He's just running away from commitment of any kind. And what really makes me crazy is that he uses the opposite argument for keeping me away. He says there'd be no career for me there, so I have to go. But there's no career for him there and he gets to stay."

"Well, you would go nuts not working," Jessie pointed out fairly, but she wrote down, *"4. He's not working. 5. He runs away from commitment. 6. He thinks there's no career for her there."*

"Okay, read me the list," Kate said gloomily, and Jessie did.

"Is that it?" Jessie said. "We can fix this stuff."

"No, there's another one," Kate said. "He doesn't want to get married. And I do. I want it all. Commitment, rings, the church, the whole thing."

"Okay," Jessie said and wrote down, *"7. He doesn't*

want to get married.'' She shoved the list across to Kate. ''Piece of cake.''

Kate looked at her in disbelief. ''Jessie, this is awful. What do you mean, piece of cake?''

''Well, you're going to have to do some compromising,'' Jessie said. ''If the man doesn't want a career, he doesn't want a career.''

Kate frowned and said, ''Maybe. What about the rest?''

Jessie pulled the list back and studied it. ''Well, number one really is easy. He won't call? You call him.''

''And sit and listen to his embarrassed silence on the other end? No.''

''Then go down and see him. It's only a four-hour drive. You miss Nancy. Penny's down there. It's been a month. Go visit.''

''I don't know…'' Kate said.

''Do you want him or not?'' Jessie snapped.

Kate thought about Jake, about how good it felt just to be with him, about how right she felt whenever he was around. ''I want him,'' she said.

''Great,'' Jessie said. ''Now number two. He thinks he might love you.'' She looked up at Kate. ''It's been a month. He may know for sure by now.''

''Which is why he hasn't called,'' Kate said. ''I hate this list.''

''Do you love him?'' Jessie demanded.

Kate swallowed and said, ''Yes.''

''Well, you haven't called him, either,'' Jessie said. ''Silence does not necessarily indicate a lack of interest. He could just be as big a chicken about this as you are.''

''Chicken?'' Kate said, but Jessie moved on down the list.

"Now, number three, he's going to have to give in on. I mean, you either confront or manipulate. Personally, I favor confrontation."

"I know," Kate said. "That is abundantly clear to everyone who knows you."

"So, go down there and confront him. Tell him you love him and you're insisting on marriage."

"And when he says, 'I think I remember you, vaguely,' I can just crawl under the nearest rock."

"Stop it," Jessie said. "You know damn well he remembers you more than vaguely. Now, number four."

"I'm still not happy about numbers one, two, and three," Kate said, but Jessie said, "Number four we've already decided you're giving in on. If he doesn't want a career, he doesn't have to have one. Number five is really number seven so we'll put that off. Number six—"

"I don't remember the numbers anymore," Kate said. "What was number five?"

"Number six is a career for you down there. That we can do if we just work on it," Jessie said. "Look, you keep telling me how overworked this Will character is. And the place must be full of little craft shops and stuff like that run by people whose idea of bookkeeping is a legal pad under the register."

"Jessie, none of those things is a full-time job," Kate said.

"Not one of them, maybe," Jessie said. "But maybe all of them are."

"What?"

Jessie shrugged. "Do them all. Once people start to hear about you, they'll come in from other places, too. All of that stuff together would keep you busy enough doing freelance consulting." She sipped some coffee. "I also think you ought to buy into Nancy's bar. You need to have something to fix, and that could take years.''

"Nancy doesn't want to sell," Kate said.

"She doesn't want to sell *all* of it," Jessie said. "You could talk her into half, expanding with the money you'd put in. You could convince her."

"That wouldn't be right," Kate said. "It's her bar. It wouldn't be right for me to try—"

"It's good for the bar. It's good for Nancy. And it's good for Toby's Corners," Jessie said flatly. "Stop being such a wimp. Do it."

"Carl Avery of Woolf Technologies, line three," Kate's secretary said, and Kate groaned and picked up the line.

"Kate! Darling, how are you?"

"What do you want, Carl?" Kate said. "I've been talking to morons all morning. I have no patience left."

"Well, then, I'll get right to the point," Carl said cheerily. "This dividend you wanted us to pay? Bad idea, Katie girl. Very bad. I'll just pencil that out, what say?"

"Over my dead body," Kate said, taking her pen back from Jessie. "Your stockholders are due a dividend. Pay it."

"Kate." Carl chuckled. "Kate, Kate, Kate."

"Carl," Kate said, tapping her pen hard against her desk, "pay it or I'll put you on my SEC Christmas-gift list."

"Kate," he said with much less enthusiasm, "this is not good business. That's what we pay your firm for— good business advice."

"Carl," Kate said, "what you want to do is morally repugnant and marginally illegal. This is good business advice."

"I'll talk to your father," Carl said abruptly.

"Good idea," Kate said. "Maybe he'll send me to bed without my supper. Who do you think you're kidding?"

But Carl had already hung up. ·

"I'm telling you," Jessie said, "Toby's Corners is full of Debbies. And no Vandenburgs except on the golf course. And no— Who was the moron on the phone?"

"Carl Avery," Kate said. "A long-standing client and potential felon."

"Well, there are no Carl Averys in Toby's Corners, either." Jessie finished her fritter and licked the sugar off her fingers. "You could help little businesses and make Nancy's bar famous—"

"Maybe Nancy doesn't want a famous bar," Kate said.

"Well, she's going to get one. Which brings us to number seven," Jessie said. "Marriage and commitment."

"Ouch. That is the big one," Kate said, wincing. "Are you sure we solved one through six?"

"Shut up," Jessie said. "You're going to have to propose."

"No," Kate said.

"Yes," Jessie said. "If you want something in life, you have to go after it. If Jake is allergic to marriage, you're just going to have to make the first move."

"He'll say no," Kate said. "You don't know Jake."

"No, but I know you," Jessie said. "And no man in his right mind would say no to you."

"Jake's not in his right mind."

"He loves you."

"Maybe," she said, and Jessie groaned.

"Look," she said. "This is your choice. Are you going

to choose to be happy with Jake and Nancy and Penny down south, or miserable with Vandenburg, Avery, and Whatsis up here?''

"Well, if I stay up here I have you, too," Kate pointed out.

"No, you don't," Jessie said. "If you walk away from this, I'm never speaking to you again."

"Let me see that list again," Kate said, and Jessie handed it to her. Kate brushed the fritter sugar off it and studied it. It was a lousy list, but it was doable. "All right," she said. "I'll do it."

Jessie shoved the phone toward her so fast it almost skidded off the desk. "Call Nancy. Buy into that bar."

"Now?"

"Of course, now," Jessie said. "Let the company pay for the call. Do it."

Kate froze, staring at the phone. "Just like that. Change my whole life, just like that."

"Yeah, just like that. What the hell." Jessie looked at Kate closely. "You look strange. Are you okay?"

"I'm terrified," Kate said. "I don't think this—"

"Don't be dumb," Jessie said. "This will be a piece of cake. Trust me. Call Nancy." Jessie picked up Kate's fritter and waved it at the phone before she bit into it. "I'm telling you, call Nancy."

Kate thought for a moment, picked up the phone, and began to dial. She bit her lip while the phone rang, and then said brightly, "Nancy?"

"Kate? At last," Nancy said. "I've been calling and calling."

"You have?" Kate said. "My secretary didn't—"

"We didn't have your business number. I've been calling you at home for the past two days. You have at least five messages on your machine. Don't you ever go home?''

"Well, lately only to sleep," Kate said. "What's wrong? Is Jake okay?"

"No," Nancy said. "You're not answering your phone. He thinks you're either dead or with another man, and he's not sure which he'd hate more. Will and I have been pushing the 'other man' theory.''

"Why?" Kate said, confused.

"Motivation," Nancy said. "He's miserable without you, but he won't do anything about it, so we're hoping jealousy will goose him into action. If he shows up at your front door screaming, 'Where is he?' you can thank us.''

Kate started to laugh. "He misses me?" she said. "He really does?"

"Well, he won't admit it, but believe me, 'misses you' is an understatement. We're thinking of having him committed. He even insulted Mrs. Dickerson. He's really miserable. I think you'd better come back and save him.''

"Well, actually, that's what I called about," Kate said. "Not saving Jake, but coming back. I'd like to—" she took a deep breath "—I'd like to buy into the bar. But not manage it," she added hastily. "Not get in your way. I wouldn't.…"

"Go ahead, get in my way," Nancy said. "I think it's a great idea. I've been going over that master plan you made. I like it. Move back here and we'll do it."

"You've been going over the plan?" Kate said. "That's wonderful." Kate blinked her surprise at Jessie, who said, "I told you so," around a mouthful of fritter. "That's terrific," Kate said. "I'm stunned. I guess great minds do think alike."

"It wasn't actually my great mind at first," Nancy said. "It was Jake's."

"Jake's?" Kate's voice broke with surprise.

"Yeah. He's spent the past couple of weeks in here every night, explaining to me about how much better my life would be if you were here." Nancy laughed. "I've seen transparent excuses before, but this one was practically invisible. He wants you back. Bad."

A couple of weeks. Jake had been thinking about this for a couple of weeks, leaving her in hell.... "Well, why isn't he calling me, then?" Kate demanded.

"I don't know," Nancy said. "I don't explain Jake. Come down here and ask him. And bring money. Your half of this dump is not going to come cheap. We're going to get you so invested in this place that you're never going to leave again."

"I'm already that invested in that place," Kate said. "But if I've been sitting up here miserable for six weeks while Jake's been sitting down there miserable for six weeks just because he didn't want to call and tell me he'd made a mistake, there's going to be hell to pay."

"Pay me first," Nancy said, "because there's definitely going to be hell to pay."

When Kate hung up a few minutes later, Jessie was finishing the last of the fritter. "So let's go to your place and I'll help you pack," she said to Kate as she licked her fingers. "We can have you on the road by nightfall."

"No," Kate said. "I have Vandenburg, Avery, and Davis to shove onto someone else. I have to fax my father my resignation and I'm not even sure where he is right now—Hong Kong, I think. I have to call a real-estate agent to sell my condo. I have to convert most of my investments to cash. And I have to decide about how I'm going to handle this list with Jake.''

"Don't delay," Jessie said. "If you delay, you will back out.''

"I can't back out," Kate said, staring into space trying to decide whether she was delighted or horrified. "I just bought half a bar.''

One week later, Jake sat in the hotel office, staring into a computer screen while his fingers danced over a numeric keypad. He was so mesmerized by what he was doing that he didn't hear the door open.

Kate stood in the office doorway for a moment, amazed. The only thing she'd ever seen Jake do with that sort of absorption before was make love to her. That reminded her of why she was there. She closed the door behind her and sat down in the chair across the desk from him and tried to remember that Nancy had said that he wanted her back, and that Jessie had said all she had to do to be happy for the rest of her life was to confront him.

With her list.

She looked at him, haloed in the lamplight, and she knew she didn't want to confront him; she wanted to crawl into his lap. He looked big and broad and safe and like everything she'd ever wanted.

And he hadn't even noticed she was there yet.

"Hello," she said loudly. Jake looked up, startled.

They stared at each other for a moment while Kate waited for him to ask her what she was doing there.

"Hi," Jake said. He started to say something else and stopped.

Another moment passed before Kate said, "I suppose you're wondering what I'm doing here."

And he said, "No. I'm just glad you're here. You look great."

"Thank you," Kate said. "So do you."

They stared at each other for another moment. *Come on,* Kate told herself. *Get this over with. Confront him.* "I bought into Nancy's bar," she began.

And Jake said, "I know. She told me. Last week. I think it's great."

"Oh," Kate said. "Well, that means I'll be moving down here. In fact, I'm here."

"That's great," Jake said again.

They stared at each other again, and finally Kate gave up. What was the point of confronting him. He didn't care, anyway. He was just sitting there, saying, "Great," like a big dummy. Anger, confusion, and misery warred in her, and anger won.

"I think I'll be going," Kate said tightly, standing, and Jake sprang up and said, "Wait a minute."

"I've been waiting six weeks," Kate snapped. "That's long enough."

"You've only been here ten minutes," Jake said. "Don't exaggerate."

"I've been gone six weeks," Kate said. "You didn't call. Did you even notice I was gone?"

"Of course, I noticed," Jake said. "It was awful."

"Six weeks," Kate said. "Six miserable, lonely, horrible weeks."

"Hey, I was miserable, too," Jake said.

"Then why didn't you call?" Kate yelled.

"Well, I was thinking," Jake began.

"You were thinking? For six weeks, you were thinking? Do you know how miserable I've been for the six weeks you've been thinking?''

"See?" Jake said reasonably. "This is why I hate this kind of stuff."

Kate began to pound on the desk. "Do you have any idea how awful it's been? I've cried for you, damn it. And I never cry."

"Kate…" Jake began, appalled.

"Six weeks!" Kate yelled. "And don't think I moved down here to chase you, either. I hate it in the city, and I love it here, and I'd move here even if you weren't here!"

"Well, see," Jake said soothingly. "That's something else we've got in common."

"We have nothing in common," Kate snapped and wheeled around to go out the door. Jake beat her to it by a second and stood in front of her, blocking her way. "Just give me a chance," he said.

"No," she said. "Get out of my way."

"I can't," he said, reaching for her, shaking his head. "I can't let you go again. And you love me. You cried for me. You said so."

"I'll get over you," Kate said. "In fact, I may be over you now."

"No, you're not," Jake said, and pulled her to him and kissed her.

Kate had forgotten how mind-bending Jake's kisses could be, how hot his mouth felt on hers, and how good and solid and right it felt to have his arms around her, and above all, how much she just needed to be with him. When she leaned into his kiss, she felt him relax against her, and they held each other close long after the kiss ended.

"Tell me you're not over me," Jake said.

"I'm not over you," Kate said into his chest. "I'm never going to be over you. It's my curse in life."

"Don't ever scare me like that again," Jake said fervently. "I thought you were really going to walk out."

"I was," Kate said. She took a deep breath and tried to pull away from him. "I may still. I have a list of demands."

"You can have them," Jake said, pulling her back close to him so she couldn't walk away. "All of them. Anything you want."

"You won't like them," Kate said.

"I'll live." He looked down at her and smiled, and she felt herself melting into him again. Before she could surrender completely, she pulled Jessie's list out of her pocket and shoved it at him.

"What's this?" he asked, taking it with one hand while keeping the other arm wrapped around her just in case she changed her mind, and she said, "Those are my demands. You're going to hate them."

He looked at the list and said, "You have really terrible handwriting."

"That's Jessie's," Kate said, feeling like a fool. "Give it back. It's dumb."

"No," he said and read, "'Number one: He won't call.'" He looked at Kate, confused.

"Well, you didn't call," Kate said.

"I'll call. I'll talk morning, noon, and night. Does it have to be on the phone?"

"Give me the list." Kate said, reaching for it but he held it out of her grasp.

"'Two: He thinks he might love her,'" Jake read. "Why does this list make no sense?"

"You said you only thought you loved me," Kate said. "It was a worry."

"Your worries are over," Jake said, looking at her with such certainty that she was stunned. "I'm nuts about you."

"Oh," Kate said.

He went back to the list. "'Three: He hates confrontation and manipulation,'" he read. "Well, that's true enough. What's the problem?"

"You're going to have to choose one or the other or we won't be talking much," Kate said. "Do you want me to confront or manipulate?"

Jake sighed. "Confront. You will anyway. What's number four? 'He's not working.'" He wiggled his eyebrows at her. "Want to bet? Come here." He drew her around to the other side of the desk, sat down in the desk chair, and pulled her into his lap, still holding on to her. "Okay, this is iffy because it's not exactly a career. See the nice computer?"

"Yes," Kate said.

"I'm playing the market again," Jake said. "It's not a career in the finest sense of the word, but..."

"What?" Kate said and leaned forward in his lap to look at the screen.

"You were right," Jake said. "I was rotting. But I don't want to go back to the rat race. So I thought I'd just stay here and be a slow rat. And maybe, someday, maybe, I'll try Templeton Financial Services. Like it?"

"I'm amazed," Kate said, and Jake pulled her back close to him while he looked at the list.

"'Five: He runs away from commitment.'" Jake read. "Forget that. I'm committed. 'Six: He thinks there's no career for her there.' I took care of that already when I talked Nancy into the bar idea. 'Seven: He doesn't want to get married.'"

"I do," Kate said. "I really do. Rings, in a church, the whole thing."

"Good," Jake said. "I spent a lot of money on these." Taking a deep breath and holding her close to him with one arm, he opened a desk drawer and pulled out a small ring box.

"Rings?" she said, sitting up away from him again as he handed her the box. "You bought rings? You didn't call me for six weeks, but you bought rings?"

"I wanted to have them when I proposed," Jake said, watching her as she opened the box. "I do not enjoy this stuff, and I thought that maybe I could just hand them to you and you'd be so stunned…"

"I am stunned," Kate said, looking at the rings. There were two carved wedding bands and a solitaire.

"There's more," Jake said. "I bought a house."

"A house," Kate said. "You bought rings and a house."

"It's just an old cottage on the lake," Jake said, looking worried. "Did I screw up again?"

"You bought a house," Kate said. "What are you going to do with the house and the rings if I don't say yes?"

"Don't even joke about that," Jake said fervently. "I've been having nightmares about that."

"Propose," Kate said.

"Will you marry me?" Jake said.

"Yes," Kate said and put the solitaire on her finger.

Jake pulled her back close to him and said, "Thank you," with such heartfelt gratitude and relief that Kate was amazed all over again.

"You really do want this," she said.

"I really do want this," he said.

"Then why six weeks…" she began, and this time he interrupted her.

"Listen, I know you're sure about this, but you're sure about everything," he said, his voice filled with love and concern. "I'm not sure about anything. I worry. And let's face it, it's not always going to be easy with us."

"I know," Kate said.

"I wanted to be sure when I asked you," Jake said, looking at her with more love than she could bear. "And now, I'm sure."

"Oh," Kate said and swallowed. "I still can't believe you bought a house and ring and let me cry for six weeks. Don't ever—"

"That's what I mean," Jake said. "I don't think I ever will, but I just didn't know how to ask you. I didn't even know how after I was sure. Look how badly I handled this. And we're going to hit this again. I will try my best, but I'll screw up and you'll fly off the handle and we'll fight."

Kate swallowed again. "I know."

"But the important thing for me," he said, looking into her eyes, "is that whatever problem we have, we can solve, because nothing will ever be as bad for me as being away from you. Nothing."

"Oh," Kate said.

"Kate?" Jake asked when she'd been quiet for a while.

"I'm just overwhelmed," Kate said, trying not to cry. "I thought I'd come back here and you might be glad to see me, and you might tell me you thought you loved me but you weren't sure, and you might even reluctantly marry me, but I never thought…"

Jake held her tighter. "Have I been that big a jerk? I thought you knew—"

"No," Kate said. "But I do now. Now that you've told me." She flashed her solitaire in the lamplight and then looked at it more closely. "These carvings. On the band. Are these fish?" she asked finally in a strangled voice.

"I had to have them made specially," Jake said.

"Fish?" Kate asked again, looking at him and loving him so much, she was almost paralyzed by it.

"Some of our best moments were in front of the fish," Jake said. "I didn't want to get you an ordinary ring. You're not an ordinary woman."

"Fish," Kate said. "Have I mentioned that I'm going to love you till the day I die?"

"You'd better," Jake said. "Because that's how long you're going to have me around." He waited a beat and then added, "Unless you kill me in bed. Go ahead and try. I don't mind."

Kate looked at the ring on her finger again. "I'm engaged," she said, and flashed it in the light again.

"Well, you've been that before," Jake said as she admired her ring. "That's why I think we should get married this weekend."

"What?" Kate said, startled. And when she turned her face to his, he kissed her, pulling her so close she felt like he'd never let her go. She kissed him back, loving the way his lips felt on hers, the gentle tickle of his mustache on her skin. And when he broke the kiss, she clung to him and buried her face in his shirt because it felt so good to be pressed against him, so safe to have his arms wrapped around her. He felt like home, and she'd never been there before.

"Engagements don't work with you," Jake said into her hair. "Those other guys, they waited too long. They let you get away."

"I'm not going anywhere," Kate said, turning her face up to his again. "If you think I'm leaving you, you're crazy. You proposed and I've got the fish to prove it."

"Of course, that was partly your fault," Jake went on as if he hadn't heard her. "You and your plan."

"Hey." Kate straightened. "My plan worked just fine. I got you, didn't I?"

"And I was part of your plan?" Jake grinned at her. "I don't think so. I think I hijacked you, babe. Blindsided you while you were twit-hunting. The best thing that ever happened to you was me showing up and that plan going south."

Kate started to protest and then stopped. He was smiling at her with so much cheerfully confident love that she went dizzy just looking at him. He was tall and dependable and successful at life, a guy with a great sense of humor who was terrific in bed and would love her to the point of madness to the day she died.

"What was I thinking?" she said, and relaxed back into the warm arms of the best plan she'd ever made, planning to stay there forever.